free REIN

The Steeplechase Secret

free REIN

The Steeplechase Secret

by
Jeanette Lane

Based on the original TV series created by
Vicki Lutas and Anna McCleery

Scholastic Inc.

To everyone
who likes the thrill of an
all-out gallop almost as
much as a lazy ride along
sun-dappled trails

An Island Visitor

Zoe breathed in the salty sea air and felt the breeze against her face. On impulse, she tugged off her boots and socks and dug her toes into the sand. She faced the ocean, curly wisps of hair fluttering in the wind. She closed her hazel eyes to feel the sun on her face, and—*BAM*!

"Raven!" Zoe yelped, stumbling forward. "Way to ruin the moment!" Raven, who had just playfully head-butted Zoe during her almost-perfect Zen moment, tossed his head in the air with a neigh. Zoe laughed and reached her arm around the beautiful black horse's neck. She took a deep breath and realized that *this* was the moment she had been working for—fighting for—ever since she had arrived on this small English island a couple of months earlier. Zoe leaned into Raven, giving him a hug. Raven snorted and dropped his coal-black head to rest on Zoe's shoulder.

"Hey, boy," she whispered into his tangled mane. "Isn't it great? No training. No Junior Nationals. No obligation to former owners who want you to win every competition." Zoe was referring to Raven's previous owner. Raven had been through a lot in his life: stolen as a foal and then shipwrecked, washing up on an island— the very island that was now their home. After that, he'd been horse-napped! But now he belonged to Zoe, and she belonged to him. It was the one thing of which Zoe was certain.

Maybe Raven hadn't minded the pressure of all the competitions, but Zoe was thrilled that life was back to normal—well, the new normal. Her old normal life was thousands of miles away, across a continent and an ocean, in Los Angeles, California. That's where she had lived her whole life until her mom decided to bring Zoe and her little sister, Rosie, to the island to visit their grandfather.

Zoe's mom had grown up on the island. She was used to being separated from the rest of the world, in a big, old stone house with a gorgeous garden and yard, where the only social life was at the local riding stables, Bright Fields. But surprisingly, Zoe was getting used to it, too.

Now her world revolved around Raven and Bright Fields. She'd made *horse-some* friends in Jade and Becky— together, they were Pony Squad! She'd also made a formidable frenemy in Mia, and she'd even had a couple of attempts at a proper boyfriend. First with Marcus, and then there was Pin. If things kept going well when Pin came back from Vienna, maybe they'd actually be able to make it "official" between them once and for all. Man, a lot had happened in a few months!

Zoe could hardly believe that her mom and Rosie had remained on the island just so Zoe could stay with Raven. "You really turned our world upside down, didn't you?" she said to him. As she thought about her old life, she gazed out at the ocean. A long, flat ferryboat caught her eye. Zoe hadn't seen any ferries dock at this side of the island. The ferries to the mainland usually came in at the pier, where there was an ice cream parlor and a couple of other attractions.

Zoe clucked to Raven and led him to the other side of the beach. "Let's get a better look," she said. Why would the boat be docking there? A little part of her told her she should just leave it alone. After all the drama with Raven and the horse stealers, she had promised her mom—and her dad, via Skype—that she would lie low and focus on her own responsibilities, like schoolwork—and Raven, of course. Still, Zoe could not contain her curiosity. On closer inspection, she could see a large SUV, a two-horse trailer, a bunch of building supplies like lumber and bags of sand, and many bales of hay and bags of grain.

"Looks pretty tasty, right?" Zoe said, patting Raven's neck, but she kept her eyes on the boat.

Just then, a boy walked to the bow and leaned over the railing. He wore a V-neck sweater with a crisp collared shirt and looked a couple of years older than Zoe. Soon, a man in a suit came up behind the boy and put a hand on his shoulder. Zoe wondered where they were headed. The island had several stables. What were the chances that they were bound for Bright Fields?

"We really should be getting back," Zoe said, as much to herself as to Raven. "Let's go, boy." But as she turned to go, Raven stayed put, still eyeing the ferry. He snorted.

"I know," Zoe said. "Something feels weird about it to me, too, but I'm sure it's nothing." Zoe looked at her horse, who did not seem convinced. "Not everything is a conspiracy!" she insisted, sounding a lot like her mom.

Raven sighed and dropped his head. When Zoe lightly jangled the reins and rubbed his ear, he followed. She trudged back to where she'd discarded her footwear. "Ugh! Sand in the socks is not a good feeling with boots on," she mumbled to herself. Raven whinnied as if to laugh at her. "I know, I know. Serves me right."

By the time Zoe made it back to Bright Fields, the excess sand was bugging her so much that she let her feet dangle out of the stirrups.

"If you would stay *on* the horse, where you belong, these things wouldn't happen to you, Zoe," Mia declared. "You keep forgetting that Raven and you are horse and rider. It's not like you're mates."

Zoe scowled. "Speak for yourself. You and Firefly may have that relationship, but Raven and I have a special bond," Zoe said, patting Raven's neck.

Still in the saddle, she pulled off her boot and turned it over. Just as the sand started to spill out, Raven snorted and blew a cloud of sand grains right in Mia's face. Zoe tried (only a little) to contain her laughter, and Mia stomped off.

Zoe had come to learn that Mia could be a little less insufferable when she wanted to be—nice, even— *sometimes*. She'd still probably never stop making snarky comments or acting like she always knew best. But Mia had her reasons for being, well, Mia, and Zoe just had to keep reminding herself of that.

Jade and Becky were a far more welcome sight on Zoe's return to the stables. Pony Squad sat together in the tack room as Zoe cleaned the sand off her feet. "I got to see a super-sized ferry arrive and dock all the way over by the cove," she said to her friends. "That's kind of weird, right?"

Becky's expression grew serious. She tugged on her super-tight French braid, deep in thought. "Very weird," she agreed, always willing to consider the most unlikely explanations first. Becky was, after all, a firm believer in the so-called ghost pony who haunted the island. "Maybe it's a pirate boat! Or a boat full of *ghost* pirates! Or a gravy boat! Wait, that's not right . . ."

Jade, as usual, opted for a rational explanation instead. "Maybe the other pier was too crowded? It does get quite busy at this time of year." Just then, Mia waltzed into the tack room with Susie, her second in command, at her flank. In her hand Mia held a fancy cream-colored envelope embossed with a gold horseshoe.

"That ferry was just the first of many," she announced. She waved the envelope like an ornate fan. Zoe would never understand how Mia's poker-straight hair always looked salon fresh after hours at the stables. "A partnership from the mainland is investing in the old Grindlerock Racing Grounds. They're going to rehabilitate it and then sponsor a formal steeplechase event at the end of the month."

This news inspired the gasps of awe that Mia had hoped for—from everyone except Zoe.

"They're using that dock because it's better for oversized deliveries, like building equipment, trailers, and *top-ranked* European racehorses," Mia went on. She watched Zoe closely for her reaction, but Zoe didn't blink or even raise her eyebrows. "Isn't it thrilling?" Mia prompted.

"Oh, yes," Susie said on command. "Thrilling."

When Mia stared her down, Zoe finally commented. "Well, I might be thrilled, but you lost me at Grindlehock, and then you lost me again at steeplechase."

"It's *Grindlerock*," Mia corrected, "and it was once a stately racecourse that attracted tourists from the mainland every weekend of the competitive season. Of course, that was long before our time, but everyone knows it was lush and lovely."

"This is an island," Zoe stated. "We've ridden all over

the place. How is there a big, fancy racetrack here that I've never seen?"

"Well," Mia replied, "Ireland and Australia are islands, too. Have you explored every square kilometer of those islands as well?"

"O-kay," Zoe replied. Mia had a point. The island did have all kinds of nooks and crannies that Zoe hadn't explored. This place was full of surprises! "But what are you so excited about, Mia? It's just a racetrack. You were a show jumper last I knew."

"Oh, Zoe," Mia said. "You are so provincially American. Steeplechase is not your stateside version of racing. It's not like the Triple Crown or other straight gallop-to-the-finish races. Steeplechase is a race with jumps. It is a quintessentially British event."

"Because they wear hats?" Zoe asked hopefully. Was there anything more British than the elegant spectator hats that they wore to weddings and parades and other posh affairs?

"Yes, because they wear hats," Mia confirmed. "And there will be hats at the Grindlerock opening event as well. You will all need one since you'll want to come cheer for Firefly and me."

"Hats? I'll make you a hat," Becky offered. "I have a

bunch of old lampshades that I've been saving for a major crafting event—I knew they'd come in handy!"

"Um, no, thanks," Mia promptly replied.

"Wait. You're racing?" Jade asked Mia. "That sounds intense."

"Well, my dad met Mr. Cooke, the event promoter, on the mainland. They hit it off, of course. When Daddy told him about my performance at Junior Nationals, Mr. Cooke asked me to compete. This is the invitation." Mia paused and raised her eyebrows for effect. "I figure we need something to focus on now that Junior Nationals are over. Who's with me?" Mia immediately turned to Zoe.

"Um, no," Zoe answered. "Raven and I need some downtime. And training for a high-profile tourist attraction with hurdles and fancy hats is anything but that."

She and Raven needed a rest. Still, it was kind of exciting, knowing that the island would host a big event in just a few weeks.

"Why don't we ride out to this old track tomorrow and see it for ourselves?" Zoe tossed her chaps into her tack trunk. "The weather's supposed to be nice, and since we don't have to train, we could take a picnic and be gone all afternoon."

"Oh! I could bake something horse-some, like carrot-cake doughnuts," Becky suggested. "They're Bob's favorite. And mine." Bob was Becky's pony.

"That sounds delicious—and fun," Jade agreed.

"I know Raven could use more time exploring and less time in the ring practicing," Zoe said, loving her plan even more. "I could, too."

"An old racing track?" Becky said absentmindedly, not seeming to have heard a word Zoe just said. "Think of all the expectations and hope over the years. The adrenaline. The rivalries. The heartbreak." She went on with a faraway look in her eyes. "I'll bet there are at least three ghost ponies trapped in the race grounds. Or maybe ghost *jockeys*," Becky whispered. Jade and Zoe turned to her. "Oh, did I say that out loud?" Becky asked, biting her lower lip.

"You did," Jade responded, giving her best friend a knowing smile. "But we'll pretend you didn't." Becky had a habit of letting her imagination get away with her. Jade preferred to stick to the facts. "We're not going on a whole ghost pony quest tomorrow. It's just a jaunt. For fun," Jade insisted. "To celebrate not having to train for Junior Nationals anymore."

Becky gave an enthusiastic smile, her braid bobbing with each nod. "Absolutely," she said. But something told Zoe that ghost ponies—or other kinds of ghosts—were still running wild in Becky's mind.

This will just be an innocent little field trip, Zoe told herself. *There won't be anything strange or mysterious at all. Right?*

2

The Grindlerock Curse

After Zoe had picked Raven's hooves, brushed the sand from his fetlocks, and given him an apple just because she liked to spoil him, she headed home—to her new decidedly British home. With the broad-leafed ivy growing up the stone front, the old manor looked like something out of a book Zoe would have to read for Advanced English Literature. Surprisingly, her grandfather's house was rather charming and cozy inside.

She found her mom and ten-year-old sister in the kitchen. Her mother was making tacos—from scratch. The island market didn't stock any of the family's preferred dinner shortcuts, and, despite the fact that her mom was filling in as a part-time manager at Bright Fields, she still had an inordinate amount of time on her hands. Back in LA, she had always been busy, tackling twelve tasks at a time and volunteering for all kinds of worthy organizations. It was harder to do that on the island, especially since the Wi-Fi connection was not the most reliable. "Zoe!" her mom exclaimed, her smile extra bright. "How was your day?"

"You seem happy to see me," Zoe said, suspicious.

"She doesn't like the way I cut the tomatoes," Rosie said, scrunching up her mouth in a pout. Unlike her mom and sister, who let their tight curls naturally frame their faces, Rosie wore her hair straightened, with soft waves. "I don't know why I should have to cut them when I don't even like them."

"Don't be ridiculous," her mother said. "You like salsa, and that is approximately eighty-five percent tomatoes."

"Well, I must really like the other fifteen percent, because I detest tomatoes," Rosie insisted.

"Here, I'll help," Zoe said, washing her hands. "Your technique is awful." She walked over to the counter and playfully nudged Rosie out of the way.

"You should help, because if it weren't for you, we'd be back in LA, and we could go to any trendy restaurant or hole-in-the-wall cantina and eat like queens," Rosie said.

"Instead, we're here so you can bond with Raven. And we have to eat Mom's food."

"Hey," Zoe's mom objected.

"Come on, Rosie, quit pretending you don't have fun at the stables, too. Why didn't you come today and ride Prince?" Prince was one of Mia's old show ponies. Mia actually liked Rosie and was letting her ride him for lessons.

"If you must know, Prince called in. He needed some 'me time,'" Rosie said. "So I obliged. And did my nails." She waved her hands in front of Zoe.

"Oh, yet another shade of pink," Zoe said. "Is that Cotton Candy Confetti?"

"How'd you guess?" Rosie asked, admiring the shiny gloss for herself.

"It's a talent," Zoe replied, slicing the tomatoes into cubes. The truth was that Zoe had stepped on the bottle that Rosie had left on the patio on her way in, spilling the shocking pink color in a small puddle. "More importantly, I have news. There's going to be some kind of race. A horse race with hurdles. They're reopening an old track and hosting a big opening-day event that will bring in tourists from all over. It's going to be in a few weeks."

"Really? Are you kidding?" Rosie's face lit up. "It's about time we got some excitement around here. Nothing ever happens. Nothing ev-er."

"How can you say that?" Zoe's mom asked with a laugh. After all, they had only been living there for a few months and they had already encountered horse thieves, a smugglers' legacy that revealed the humble stable boy was the descendant of a wealthy duke, and an impulsive proposal by their grandfather to a fortune-teller. Personally, Zoe thought it had been a rather eventful stay.

"Well, a proper horse race is more my kind of event," Rosie admitted.

"There will be hats," Zoe said. Rosie eyed her uncertainly.

"Not hard hats for riding," Zoe confirmed. "Big, colorful hats for looking sophisticated, borderline ridiculous."

Rosie gasped. "Like at the royal weddings?"

"Exactly." Zoe was happy to see her sister really smile again.

"Now this is going to be good," Rosie insisted, shuffling out of the room in her heels. "No one else get on the Internet. No slowing down the Wi-Fi. I *have* to research. I need the perfect outfit. I only get one chance to select my debut spectator hat and choose the best accompanying ensemble. Three weeks is not much time for this kind of thing!"

Zoe and her mom locked eyes and tried not to laugh out loud. "At least she's excited about something," her mom said.

"I'm excited about this dinner," Zoe said. "It looks like it's going to be good."

"It had better be. I've been chopping for an hour!" her mom replied. "So, how did you hear about this upcoming race?"

"Mia had all the news, as usual. She was apparently invited to compete by the head organizer himself," Zoe said. "She was trying to get everyone else to do it, too."

"And?" her mom prompted.

"Are you kidding? I don't know the first thing about steeplechase races," Zoe said, popping a cherry tomato into her mouth.

"Well, I have to admit, I'm glad to hear you're taking it a bit easy for once," her mom said, eyeing her daughter carefully. "Maybe that's for the best. Trouble certainly has seemed to find you easily since we moved here."

The last thing Zoe wanted was her mom worrying about her again. It wasn't that long ago that her mom hadn't even wanted her riding at all. She'd finally come around, but who's to say she wouldn't change her mind again with all the crazy things that had happened lately? "Don't worry, Mom," Zoe said quickly. "I promise, no more drama for me. I'm staying out of it—the riskiest thing I have planned is a picnic tomorrow that involves eating something Becky usually bakes for Bob."

Her mom laughed and seemed to relax. She proceeded to tell Zoe that her great-aunt Zelda had competed at Grindlerock. "I'm certain we have a picture of her around here somewhere. She was my mum's sister. Anyway, it really was the thing to do back in the day, but then there were a number of freak accidents. After a string of them, rumors started about the course being cursed."

"Oh, come on," Zoe said, rolling her eyes. "What is it about this island and tall tales?"

Her mom shook her head. "No, really. People say it's one of the reasons that Grindlerock was finally shut down," she said. "I mean, this was all long before I was born, but I heard lots of stories."

"Of course you did. This place is full of stories," Zoe said with a smile. One of Zoe's favorite parts of being in England was finding out more about her mom's own childhood.

"I won't argue with you there," her mom said. "But

I am excited about this race coming up. It seems like it could be a good distraction for Rosie. I really want for her to figure out how to fit in and enjoy living on the island." She wiped her hands on her apron and turned on the stove. "I'm sure the two of you will both have lots of fun seeing the spectacle of all of it. While still paying attention to your schoolwork, of course," she added in sudden mock-seriousness.

"Yes, that," Zoe admitted.

"And nightly family dinners," her mom added.

"And family dinners," Zoe agreed, "but only if these tacos are as delicious as they look, because I'm starving."

"I wonder why they put up this fence around the racing grounds. Perhaps they're hiding something," Becky said as she unpacked her picnic offerings and spread them out on the blanket. The journey from Bright Fields had been long but surprisingly uneventful as far as most Pony Squad outings went. Bob had not spooked at any of the squirrels or tried to herd the sheep in the Grange's meadow for once. It was a crisp autumn day, and the horses were now happily grazing nearby. "Maybe they're keeping people away because of the Grindlerock *Curse*!" Becky added, raising her eyebrows meaningfully.

Zoe had a feeling she shouldn't have repeated her mom's stories about Grindlerock on the ride over. She thought it was funny, but she should have known that Becky would take it much more seriously. "You promised Jade you wouldn't be sniffing out any of that stuff, remember?"

"Technically, I promised no ghosts," Becky pointed out. "I never said anything about no curses. But anyway, I thought they'd want everyone to see what they're up to," Becky explained, her hair looking especially blond in the afternoon sun. "They should want to get the people excited about the rebuilding of the track, you know. All the activity would be like free publicity."

Zoe had to admit what Becky said made sense. She almost sounded like a marketing executive—except for the fact that she was wearing multiple-colored hairbands and a homemade T-shirt that had HORSE-SOME airbrushed on it. But still, Zoe was disappointed—she had wanted to see what a steeplechase track looked like, but the fence was just high enough to block them from getting a good look at anything.

Meanwhile, Jade chose to ignore the topic altogether, focusing instead on their picnic.

"So, crisps, chocolate, and biscuits—or cookies, as Zoe would say," Jade said, listing Becky's contribution. "What happened to the carrot-cake doughnuts?" she asked.

Becky's cheeks immediately lost their rosy glow. "Um, I might have left them too close to Bob's stall? And I might have left the tin slightly open, so he could smell them? By accident, of course." The three girls turned to look at Bob, who certainly appeared happy.

Jade sighed. "What did you bring, Zoe?"

"Um, pretty much the same thing," Zoe admitted. "But I also have some American candy."

"I'm not sure how you two expect to ride home," Jade said, scowling. "You'll be bouncing out of your saddles on extreme sugar highs."

"So what did you bring, then? Did a nutritionist select your meal from all the food groups?" Becky asked teasingly.

Jade slowly pulled out three bags of cheddar-flavored chips, some licorice, and cans of soda. "But I did bring carrots for the horses," she said sheepishly. She held out one of the carrots to Major, her favorite horse at Bright Fields.

"At least they'll have a good meal and can get us home," Becky said, ripping into one of the bags of chips. She looked past the narrow slats of the temporary fence to where they could see a few of the course's jumps. "If the promoter for the Grindlerock Classic had seen you and Raven, he certainly would have invited you to compete as well," Becky said.

"What do you mean?" Zoe asked.

"She means that you and Raven could actually compete. With his racing bloodlines and your determination, you'd nearly be unbeatable," Jade explained.

"My determination?" Zoe repeated with a laugh. "I'm determined not to race Raven ever again. You saw what happened when we went up against Pin on the beach. That was bad news." Zoe didn't like to remember that day. "That race almost ruined my whole relationship with Raven. What we have isn't unbreakable. It's all based on trust. I had to work hard to gain it back. I don't want to jeopardize that again."

Zoe gazed over to where Raven was lazily nibbling grass, the sun beaming off his glossy black coat. Thinking about how she had disappointed him broke her heart. She had almost lost Raven, more than once. It was only because of a crazy story of hidden identities and reclaimed fortune that Pin had managed to buy him for her. Zoe knew Pin wouldn't want her to race Raven just for glory. Her thoughts were suddenly interrupted by a sharp tapping sound nearby.

"Hello!" Jade called out to a young man who was standing just on the other side of the fence, visible from the shoulders up. He was nailing up a small poster. "Are you part of the racecourse?"

"Not technically," he answered with a smile. His navy ball cap did little to shield his eyes—or his freckled nose—from the angle of the sun.

Jade let out a laugh and smiled back. "You know what I meant." Zoe and Becky exchanged glances. It wasn't often that anyone caught Jade off guard. "Are you working on the racecourse?" she revised her question.

"Yes, I am," he said. "I'm Liam. I'm on the grounds crew. We're renovating the track and old obstacles."

"That sounds interesting," Jade said.

"It is," Liam agreed after determining that her comment was genuine. "It's such a historic place. We're staying true to many of the original designs, but updating them so they're safer and meet current standards. We're trying new turf that drains well since the island gets such heavy rain. Stuff like that."

"Did you test the soil? There is a lot of peat in it at this end of the island, I think," Jade said.

"Who's Pete?" Becky whispered to Zoe. Zoe shrugged as Jade continued chattering away.

"Jade must be loving this. I don't suppose you knew that Jade gets all excited studying soil and rocks and plants and stuff. She does it in her free time," Becky explained. "For fun."

Finally, Jade turned and introduced her friends to Liam.

"Pleased to meet you," Liam said, placing his hammer so it hung from his utility belt. "Will you be competing on Opening Day?" He motioned to their horses.

"Oh, no," Becky replied. "Bob prefers the delicate rigors of dressage to the stamina challenge of steeplechase." Becky took a bite of licorice and quickly swallowed. "Bob is the paint, but you probably guessed that. He is such a *Bob*." She gestured to her pony, who was part paint horse, part draft horse, and had the long feathered hair at his fetlocks to prove it—which Zoe thought, squinting, was very possibly covered with a light dusting of doughnut crumbs.

"Zoe and I aren't racing, either," Jade said. "She rides Raven, the black horse, and I ride Major. He used to be a police horse." Her voice had a real sense of pride when she spoke about Major, who was very no-nonsense, like Jade herself. "Zoe and I do more jumping. Steeplechase seems a bit of a hazard."

"Jade prefers to be in control," Becky added.

Zoe thought Jade might be annoyed by Becky's interjection, but Jade shrugged it off. "It's true," she admitted. "Horses have died running the Grand National. It's perilous, all those hooves pounding away and lunging for the hurdles at the same time. I prefer jumping a course when only my horse and I are in the ring. I can count the strides, regulate our pace."

"Makes sense," Liam agreed. "I didn't even bring my horse. I'm letting my sister ride her while I'm away."

"So you're not from the island?" Zoe asked.

"No. I had never even heard of it until I applied for the groundskeeper internship," Liam said. "But it's very nice here. Perfect for horses."

"So," Zoe said. "Why all the fences, Liam?"

"Honestly," Liam said. "I have no idea why. We have plenty to do before the track opens. Why have the groundskeepers waste time putting up a fence that they'll have to take right down again?"

That's exactly what Zoe had been thinking. She

didn't quite share Becky's theory that the fence there was to keep people away from a curse—but it still seemed strange.

"It could be a safety thing, so no one gets hurt and sues them," Jade said, sounding as rational as ever.

"Oh, I just got a text," Liam said suddenly, glancing at his phone. "From the boss. I need to head in. It was nice meeting you all."

Hmm, Zoe thought. *He conveniently just has to leave as soon as I start asking questions?* Then she shook her head. Maybe she'd been hanging around Becky for too long! She looked over at Raven grazing under the beautiful blue sky, the hint of a sea breeze ruffling his mane. As she took in the peaceful scene, the Grindlerock Curse seemed more ridiculous than ever.

An Intriguing Invitation

*W*ell, he was nice," Jade said, turning back to the others after Liam had left.

"Sure," Becky replied, not sounding convinced.

"What?" Jade questioned.

"It's just that Zoe and I didn't have as much to talk about with him as you did," Becky said.

"That's ludicrous," Jade said. "He was very interesting. He got into horses and designing courses all on his own. His family was in the landscape business, so he knows a lot about what soils are best for the track and all. It's cool, isn't it?"

"I guess so," said Zoe, shrugging. "It would have been *really* nice if he had let us onto the grounds."

"I admit, it would've been cool to get closer and see

how they're restoring everything," Jade said. "But I don't think he's allowed to do that."

Zoe knew Jade was right. Liam seemed pretty harmless, and the fence probably was for safety reasons. She'd promised her mom she'd stay out of drama from now on, and that was what she was going to do!

"Well, since we're clearly not getting any more information about the curse, we should start heading back," Becky said.

The girls began gathering up the remains of their picnic, all feeling a little disappointed, when they heard a new voice call out.

"What are you three doing here?"

"Mia," they all mumbled together.

"You refuse to put in the effort to train for Opening Day at Grindlerock, so why bother coming all this way merely to view the grounds?" Mia demanded from atop Firefly, with Susie next to her on her own horse, Darcy.

Zoe blew the loose curls from her face, trying to decide if she should take the high road and respond maturely or snap back with some snark of her own, when Susie spoke up.

"Mia, the reopening of Grindlerock is the biggest

thing to happen here in years," she said in a dignified tone. "Even if they don't feel like they can run with the challengers from the mainland, they're still intrigued. Certainly, you understand that."

"Well, I suppose that's so," Mia responded with a huff. She sat as poised as ever on Firefly, her form looking effortless as always.

"Besides, you hardly want them representing Bright Fields if they won't do it well," Susie added for good measure.

Zoe flashed Susie a grateful smile. Susie responded with a sly smile of her own. Zoe knew that Susie didn't really mean what she had said. Susie had been so supportive of Jade and Zoe when they rode together at Junior Nationals. But, after years of being best friends, Susie knew exactly what Mia wanted to hear—and sometimes that was just easier.

"How is the course coming along?" Mia wondered out loud, riding up to the skimpy border fence.

As she stared in the distance, several figures appeared from within the fenced area. They were climbing up the grassy crest of the hill. It was a full group, headed by a man in a dapper cream-colored suit and a stylish straw hat with a satin band. At once, Zoe recognized him as the man from the ferry the day before. The teenaged boy was also there. From this distance, it was obvious that the two were related. Both had fit, athletic builds and the same clean, conservative hairstyle. Today, the boy wore a crisp Oxford shirt with jeans and paddock boots.

It was when Zoe looked behind the newcomers that she caught her breath. Four riders from Holloway followed the pair she assumed was father and son. Did this mean that Holloway was sending multiple competitors to the Grindlerock opening? And why were *they* allowed on the grounds?

Zoe turned to Mia, still mounted on Firefly, to gauge her reaction. As far as Zoe could tell, Mia wasn't concerned with Holloway, Bright Fields's strongest rivals, at all. Mia appeared to be eyeing the son, and she appeared to be impressed.

"Hello there," the man called out, tapping the brim of his hat in greeting. "Always good to see racing fans inspecting the grounds here at Grindlerock."

"Well—" Jade stepped forward, ready to let him know her opinion of steeplechase racing, but Mia dug her heels into Firefly so the gray horse grunted and pushed to the front of the Bright Fields group, cutting Jade off.

"Yes, and we're pleased with the progress of the track

thus far," Mia announced as if she had been appointed their spokesperson.

The man turned to Mia. "And do I know you?" he asked.

"Well, yes. Mr. Cooke, I assume?" Mia answered. The man raised his eyebrows. "You met my father several weeks ago at the board meeting of Franklin Brothers and Wright. Elliott MacDonald?" Mia pursed her lips and smiled in a way that seemed to lift her cheekbones, but her confidence slowly began to droop when the man did not seem to recognize her father's name. "The two of you spoke, and you sent me an invitation to compete on Opening Day. I'm Mia MacDonald." There was a slight hitch in her voice, but she tilted her head and forced another smile.

"Oh, yes, of course," Mr. Cooke responded. "He showed me video of your round at Junior Nationals. Quite impressive."

"That sounds like Dad," Mia said, her grin now reaching from ear to ear. "He can be so embarrassing, always pulling out his phone with photos and video."

"Yes, I'm sure she just *hates* the attention," Zoe whispered to Becky and Jade sarcastically. They giggled quietly.

"I'm thrilled that you will be bringing your expertise to our Opening Day event. Is this your mount for the race?" Mr. Cooke regarded Firefly.

"Why, yes," Mia replied.

"He's gorgeous." The statement came from the teenaged boy whom Zoe had seen on the boat.

"Pardon me, this is my son, Crispin," Mr. Cooke said, shifting to put his hand on Crispin's shoulder. "He will be riding our entry in the race, Supersonic." He gave his son's shoulder a squeeze.

"Pleasure to meet you," Crispin said. He first made eye contact with Mia, but then politely proceeded to recognize the others. They all shared a civil round of introductions, made awkward by the long, somewhat tortured history between the Bright Fields's riders and those hailing from Holloway.

When Mr. Cooke realized that Mia was the only rider from Bright Fields planning to take part in the race, he looked shocked. "Well, that won't do," he declared, his thin, dark eyebrows coming together in a scowl. "One of our main objectives in rehabilitating the track is for the enjoyment of the locals. I was hoping far more of you would get to take part." He looked skyward, thinking. "Maybe, instead of racing, you'd like to come and have a practice go on the course before we raise the fences. It would be a prime way for you to see the course, and it would give our groundskeepers a way to assess how the course is progressing."

Zoe had to admit that that sounded amazing. The reaction of everyone else, Jade included, suggested they agreed.

"Then it's decided," Mr. Cooke declared magnanimously. "We will meet back here in a week's time, and you can experience the elegance and excitement of Grindlerock for yourselves."

The Bright Fields riders were all won over by Mr. Cooke's generosity. What could be more fun than bounding across the green countryside, effortlessly jumping fences, without the pressure of judges or timers? And better yet, they'd get to tour the course with their friends!

"But it's just for fun," Mia said as she was tacking up Firefly a few days later. She was getting ready to train, while the others were going for a ride to the beach. Mia brushed some sawdust from the back of her saddle, refusing to look at the others. "Why would you want to just do the course for fun? Why don't you want to ride it to win?"

Zoe buckled her helmet and gave Mia an incredulous look. "We want to do it for fun"—Zoe paused for effect—"because it's *fun*."

"Solid point," Becky chimed in. Mia had, for admittedly brief moments, proven herself to be a real team player when it came to representing Bright Fields. But her motives for riding in the Grindlerock Classic seemed self-absorbed at best.

"Even if I wanted to race, I wouldn't be able to pay that entry fee," Becky said, absentmindedly braiding Bob's mane as per her usual habit. "It's astronomical."

"But look at the prize money," Mia said. "It's impressive. We could really spruce up Bright Fields with those funds."

"Um," Susie began, "are you going to give a portion of the winnings to Bright Fields if you win?"

"I might." Mia fidgeted with her reins while everyone stared at her in disbelief. "Well, I could," she declared defensively.

"Most likely you wouldn't," Susie said. "I think you'd expect your dad to take you to Paris."

"Forget Paris," Mia scoffed. "I'd insist on Fiji, or Abu Dhabi."

"That's the Mia we know and love," Zoe said.

"Please," Mia responded. "If you loved me you'd help me prepare for the race. No one has even signed up to be my guest trainer. I've had slots open all week. You could have designed courses for me or asked me to post without stirrups. I would have done it." Zoe bit her lip. She had not even considered the joy of forcing Mia to do a full lesson without stirrups! Of course, Mia's form was so good that it probably wouldn't be much of a trial for her anyway.

"And you all laughed when I offered to bring in enough ingredients so that everyone could take part in the juice cleanse that I'm doing before the Classic," Mia continued. "I just wanted you to feel included in my prep work."

"Mia, we can't all do a juice cleanse at the same time," Susie pointed out as she tightened Darcy's girth. "We only have one loo."

Zoe, Becky, and Jade laughed. Susie caught Mia's glare and returned an innocent smile, a twinkle in her clear blue eyes. Only Susie could get away with such an honest response.

"Still," Mia huffed. "Well, at least Marcus is willing to school me over the fences," she said, pulling herself into her custom-made saddle and heading for the ring.

"Of course, it is his job," Jade pointed out, her eyes darting to Mia's back to make sure she hadn't overheard.

"I suppose I'll find you all reclining on the hay bales when I'm finished," Mia called out wistfully as she rode away. "I'll be too fatigued to join in the petty gossip."

Becky raised the back of her hand to her forehead with dramatic flair.

The four remaining riders headed out to the open meadow. Zoe was certain Raven would be excited for another lazy stroll through the fields and along the beach, but as they walked past the schooling ring, Raven veered toward the open gate. His ears were pricked as Firefly did a figure eight across the arena at a quick trot. "Not today, boy," Zoe said, eyeing the water jump and the in-and-out combination fences. Marcus had set up a challenging course, and Zoe found herself automatically thinking about how she would navigate it, where she'd make her turns. Raven pulled his head toward the ring, whickering softly. "C'mon, we're going for a trail ride and to the beach," Zoe said, but Raven did not respond to her voice as usual. Zoe pressed lightly with her heels on his sides, but he stayed put and even stamped a front hoof as if in protest. Zoe pushed her seat into the saddle and squeezed with both legs, raking her heels against his sides. She rarely had to use all her cues to move him forward. Finally, Raven relented with a snort and a lazy step toward Jade, Becky, Susie, and their horses.

Fashion and Fishy Fences

*M*ia!" Rosie called from the edge of the ring. Even though Zoe had tried her best to tempt her, Rosie had opted to stay at the stables rather than take Prince to the beach with the others. She had a far more important mission that afternoon. "Mia!" Rosie called again, stepping onto the bottom rail of the fence and waving.

"She has to clear one more course before she's done with her lesson, Rosie," Marcus advised from the center of the ring. "You'll have to wait." Rosie sighed. "And don't you have a lesson in a half hour?" he added.

"I'm not sure Prince is up for it today," Rosie said. "He looks kind of sick."

"No," Marcus said, turning to face her head-on. "He's

just dirty. Get out the currycomb and put some wrist into it. I know your arms can do more than wave."

Rosie's jaw dropped. None of her other extracurricular teachers—ballet, clothing design, flower arranging—had ever spoken to her like that! Who did Marcus think he was? Did he forget that she had once stood up for him and taken his side when he was Zoe's boyfriend? So ungrateful.

"Rosie, you have a lot of natural potential as a rider," Marcus said, his voice softening. "You could be a talented equestrian, but not if you don't ever get on a horse."

Rosie scowled. She wanted to dismiss what he said, but Marcus looked very earnest, standing there in his breeches and high boots. Maybe he was right.

"Seriously, Prince. What do you do? Escape from your stable, roll in the muck heap, come back, and lock yourself in again?" Rosie asked, aiming her interrogation at a manure stain on the pony's hindquarters. She was attempting to brush Prince clean when Mia appeared at the stall door.

"What's that on your face?" Mia asked.

"This old thing? It's just an embroidered silk scarf I got at a vintage shop," Rosie confessed. "Surely not what it's intended for, but I need something to keep the clouds of dirt away. It's like a dust bowl in here. I think I'm allergic." She wagged her fingers to clear the air around her eyes.

"Well. I'm certain this is not why you interrupted my training this afternoon," Mia said, sounding put out.

As if a five-alarm bell had gone off in her head, Rosie yanked the scarf down and gave Mia a winning grin. "No, I interrupted you on a matter of quintessential style. I'm certain you know there's a Race Day Banquet before the Grindlerock Classic, because you're Mia," Rosie said, laying it on heavily. "You know everything."

Mia actually blushed.

"I need to know what you are wearing," Rosie said. "And, if possible, I'd like to help curate your look."

"Go on," Mia prompted.

"It's just my opinion, but I believe your dress and hat for the banquet should match the colors of your racing silks."

Rosie had Mia's full attention now. At last! Someone was taking her participation in the race seriously. Mia had been so concerned with training that she had not considered the fun in being part of the fanfare as well. "Wait," Mia said, coming to her senses. "You're American. What do you know about ornate hats?"

"Please," Rosie said, rubbing her nose and leaving a streak of dirt on her cheek. "Half of my family is British, remember? Not that Brits always get style right, anyway—have you seen how my grandfather wears tweed? Absolute overkill."

"Very well," Mia said. "Get to the point."

Rosie launched into her style plan for Mia, describing a wide-brimmed hat with organza flower embellishments, or possibly live flowers, and a simple high-waisted dress. "Of course, if it were winter, I'd have to endorse an over-sized beret in a neutral shade," she added, "but I've always been partial to modern updates to classics." Rosie hardly even realized that, as she spoke, she was using steady, circular strokes with the curry brush and attacking all Prince's caked-on patches of dirt with determination and polished grooming skill.

"You are super lucky that Firefly has such a lovely gray coat," Rosie continued. "It's so much better for the bold color palette that is so popular in racing today."

"Not just today," Mia corrected. "Every day. It's

tradition, and bright colors are easier for spectators to see from far away."

"So does that mean you'll let me help you?" Rosie said eagerly. "Please, don't let my talents be wasted during the biggest event this little sliver of land has ever seen!"

Mia grinned. "All right," she agreed.

Between school, house chores, riding, and tasks around the stable yard, Zoe barely had time to sleep, let alone to think about Pin and wonder what he was up to in Vienna. Still, it wouldn't hurt if the boy would check in now and again! Zoe knew he wasn't the type to post countless photos of himself riding Lipizzaner horses all over social media. He also wasn't going to text Zoe a picture of every Viennese torte he saw and tell her it reminded him of her, because they were both sweet. Zoe didn't want those things from him. They were too obvious, and they weren't at all *Pin*. Still, she wouldn't mind a postcard. A quick text. Maybe one a day—two, max.

It seemed weird to have all the Grindlerock

excitement happening without him. Zoe knew he never would have competed, even though he would have been amazing at it. But he would have loved the chance to tour the course—or maybe even help restore it, like Liam. As Zoe rode to the entrance where Mr. Cooke was meeting them, she wished Pin could be there, too.

When they arrived at the majestic, centuries-old iron gate, it was the younger Mr. Cooke who greeted them. It was the first time Zoe had seen him in riding breeches and high boots. He looked so at ease in them, Zoe couldn't remember seeing him in anything else. He was on foot but held the reins of a gorgeous chestnut horse with a wide stripe that plunged from the top of its head to its nostrils. With elegant legs, muscular hindquarters, and a radiant coat, the horse was truly striking.

"Good afternoon, everyone," Crispin said. "Welcome." The group from Bright Fields said all the appropriately gracious lines about the special opportunity. Crispin responded with polite nods and a stately smile. As soon as he had closed the gate behind them, Crispin mounted his horse.

"And who is this lovely creature?" Mia asked, her voice like velvet.

"This is my dad's pride and joy," he said. "Mia, meet Supersonic."

"Mia's good at that," Becky whispered to the others.

"At what?" Zoe asked, also in a confidential whisper.

"At talking to boys," Becky clarified, looking over her shoulder as she gathered Bob's reins. "I've only just transitioned from grunts to almost half sentences around Hot Marcus." Her arched eyebrows dipped into a sudden scowl. "Is it odd that they act like they've known each other for years?"

Susie took in the coquettish back-and-forth between Mia and Crispin. It looked fairly typical to her. "Mia said her dad got along famously with Mr. Cooke. They even talked about going into business together," Susie explained. "Fine with me if she takes care of cozying up with our host. Then we can enjoy the course!"

They rode down a narrow trail that led to a tremendous stretch of green meadow. Along one side was a grandstand, for the spectators. Two workers were busy giving it a bright white coat of paint. A luxury box, complete with a stately ivy-green canopy, was located toward the end.

"The race will finish down there," Crispin told them, "where the Holloway riders are waiting."

All the Bright Fields riders tightened their reins as if by shared instinct. The history between the two stables was tense at best. At worst, it was vindictive and emotionally treasonous. Some of the Holloway riders would do anything to win.

When they met up with the Holloway riders, Crispin launched into an explanation of the grounds. "Grindlerock is unusual in its design, the way it combines different racing styles. The opening is a traditional steeplechase, which leads into the cross-country course, and then the final push is a straight gallop to the finish line. It's part of why it's such a fun go for the riders—and the horses. It's also one of the reasons I'm so excited that we're restoring it. The track actually holds a unique place in England's racing history, and it deserves to be back in business."

The course was not a giant oval where spectators could watch from the center, like the American racetracks Zoe had seen sometimes on TV back in LA. Here, the crowd could gather all along the track to see the different sections of the race, with the grandstand offering the prime view of the finish line.

"I think the best way to get a sense of the track is to ride it," Crispin said.

"Like, right now?" Zoe asked, suddenly feeling a bit nervous. This track was no joke.

"What's the matter, Zoe? Haven't given Raven his minty bribe yet?" Callum, one of the Holloway riders—and Susie's ex-boyfriend—asked with a chuckle.

Zoe's eyes flashed with annoyance. Callum had a lot of nerve, bringing up her habit of giving Raven mints—especially after Holloway's trainer had tried to drug her mints at Junior Nationals to ensure that Holloway would end up with the win.

"I don't think you want to get into who plays fair and who doesn't, Callum," Zoe said, taking a deep breath.

"You've obviously lost your nerve," chirped another Holloway rider. "We noticed that you aren't competing in the Classic on Opening Day."

Zoe's lower jaw jutted out as she tried to suppress her frustration. "That has nothing to do with anything other than Raven and I just don't want to race," Zoe said, keeping her tone as even as possible.

"Well, yeah. That's kind of proof that you lost your nerve," the girl declared.

"Now, now," Crispin cut in. "The best way to solve minor disagreements is on the track. Am I right?" Without another word, he bumped Supersonic's sides with his heels and the horse surged forward. With no more than a click of Mia's tongue, Firefly was on Supersonic's tail. Mia's laugh trailed in the air behind her. Callum and the other Holloway riders took off as well.

Susie, Jade, Becky, and Zoe looked at one another and shook their heads. "I'm in no rush," Zoe said, noting that she had Raven's reins looped tight in her hands. "I'm looking for a leisurely jaunt. Sightseeing, if you will." Raven stamped his hoof and snorted.

"I'm not even doing the jumps," Becky said, waving her hand at the course as if it were a heap of moldy manure. "As you know, Bob would prefer to limbo under rather than leap over. It's just his way."

"Well, I've decided the topic for my big journalism project," Jade announced. "I'm doing it on Grindlerock, so I'm not rushing through the course. This is research!" Jade looked thrilled.

Raven stamped his front hoof and snorted again. "Okay, boy. You've waited long enough," Zoe said. "Let's get going, everyone. After all, this is a racecourse." As soon as Zoe shifted in the saddle, Raven leaped forward as if he were released from a starting gate. In three ecstatic strides, they had left the others far behind. "Whoa," Zoe yelped in shock. After the initial surprise wore off, she let Raven find his own pace. She heard Jade and Susie call to her, but she let Raven keep his rhythm. She'd slow him down after they'd taken a few fences and he showed signs of tiring.

But Raven didn't tire. Zoe felt him grow stronger as they approached each hurdle, his legs easily clearing the hedgerow fences that stretched across the wide grass track. Zoe knew the fences were now a fraction of the height that they'd be for Opening Day, but Raven jumped as if he could clear a hurdle three times as high.

In no time, they had moved into the second phase of the track, cross-country—which was trickier. There were more twists and turns and slopes—and Zoe knew that they were certain to encounter the inevitable, stressful water fence. Raven had come a long way when dealing with any water obstacle, but Zoe knew they always had to work together carefully to time their takeoffs.

"Steady, boy," Zoe said as they entered a wide gully. Raven's ears flicked around and he raised his head, shortening his stride. "What is it?" Zoe asked, leaning forward. Raven lifted his nose and whinnied, shrill and long. Zoe finally realized that there was indeed a water fence up ahead—a wide pool of water with thick green hedges on the far side. High wooded ridges rose on either side of the track. The trees blocked out the sun, leaving the water jump in a dim haze. The jump seemed to be closing in on them, even though the track was almost as wide on the rest of the course. But the ground was uneven underfoot. It had a marked pitch that lured Raven to the left, to the lower part of the water fence. "Steady, steady," Zoe reassured Raven, holding tight on the right rein. Zoe sat back in the saddle, trying to even Raven's pace and keep him toward the center of the jump. Raven pulled against Zoe, but Zoe held strong. The far side of the fence felt too close to the ridge, and Zoe didn't like the slope.

If they were racing, it would make sense to hug the ridge and make a tighter turn. But they weren't racing. And Raven already had an issue with water. She didn't want Raven to have to scramble over the obstacle. As wide as it was, he'd need amazing speed to clear it. Zoe held her right rein tight and pushed hard against Raven with her left leg. Three, two, one more stride and they leaped over the jump.

Raven lowered his head and gave it a shake, and Zoe let out a sigh of relief. "We made it," she said, looking over her shoulder at the fence from the other side, trying to shake a feeling of unease. "We made it," she repeated, letting Raven gallop out of the shady gully into the open air. "Whoa, boy, whoa," she said, pulling hard on the reins. She sat back and took a deep breath. She'd wait for the others there.

A Surprise Announcement

Zoe was glad to have company for the rest of the course. The water fence had rattled her a bit, and she wasn't sure why.

Susie and Jade chatted as they made their way over the other cross-country obstacles. They had the air of a couple of friends strolling around a lake. Their horses were relaxed in a smooth, easy canter.

Raven did not pick up on the other horses' mellow moods. No matter what Zoe did, she could not get him to settle down. Even though she and Raven kept pace with Jade's and Susie's horses, Raven pulled against Zoe, his stride fast and choppy. He worked himself into a sweaty lather. Zoe had fun, but it was not the leisurely ride she had been anticipating. Maybe the racing in Raven's blood had taken over!

When they all arrived at the end of the course, Zoe could tell that Mia and the Holloway riders had not considered it a leisurely ride, either, but for other reasons. For Mia and the others who were competing in the Grindlerock Classic, it had not been a sightseeing tour; it was a practice round before the main race, even if the fences were shorter. The riders had now taken off their saddles, letting their horses cool off before the long ride home.

Becky came trotting up shortly after Jade, Susie, and Zoe finished.

"Did you enjoy your relaxed ride around the grounds?" Jade asked.

"As if," Becky said, her eyes wide. "When you have to go around the fences, you see some unexpected sights."

"What do you mean?" Susie asked.

"I mean, when you have to go around the fences, you see some things you didn't expect to see," Becky replied mysteriously, giving the girls a meaningful look.

"Well, what surprised you?" Zoe asked, hoping Becky would spit it out already.

Becky shuddered. "I wouldn't say it surprised me. I've

been suspicious of this place from the start. With the curse and all, you know."

"What was it?" Jade asked, with growing impatience.

"Well, you know that water fence that's in a kind of ravine, with the steep hills on both sides?" Becky asked.

Zoe nodded, rustling Raven's mane. That was the jump that had made her and Raven uneasy.

"I couldn't just walk around it. It's like a trap, so Bob and I had to go all-terrain, uphill, and trailblaze through all these trees and tumbleweed."

"Um, I'm pretty sure tumbleweed only grows in the desert," Jade said.

Becky waved her hand as if that was a minor detail. "Anyway, Bob and I were skirting a big patch of tumbleweed when we noticed a man in a tan suit and sunglasses, holding binoculars. He was motioning to someone. I looked across to the other hill, on the other side of the water fence, and there was another man, dressed just like the first man, also with binoculars." Becky got a far-off look as she recounted the event, then suddenly her eyes widened as if she had realized something. "Maybe they're responsible for the curse! Maybe they're twin ghosts who have cursed the grounds for eternity!"

"Ghosts?" Jade screeched, then pursed her lips,

suddenly aware of her extreme volume. She glanced around to make sure she hadn't attracted unwanted attention. She traded looks with Zoe and Susie. "Ghosts?" she said again, this time in a whisper. "What about two men in suits makes you think 'ghosts'?"

"You didn't see them," Becky insisted. "Something wasn't right with them, I know it. And I'm not just talking about their super-weird outfits."

Zoe smirked. While she was not one hundred percent behind Becky's theory, she had to agree that there was something spooky about that fence. Raven clearly had agreed, too.

"Maybe your article should be called 'The Ghosts of Grindlerock,'" Becky suggested to Jade. "Or 'The Truth Behind the Grindlerock Curse.'"

"Hmmm, maybe not," Jade replied. "It's supposed to be a fact-based piece with quotable resources. I'm not jeopardizing my grade by entertaining speculation about specters."

Zoe stifled a laugh. Becky looked slightly hurt.

"Sorry, Becky," Jade said quickly "I didn't mean that to sound so harsh. I guess it is kind of weird that there were guys with binoculars up there, but I'm sure they just wanted to see how the horses handled the course.

They want to get it just right for Opening Day. I'll ask Liam about it when I interview him for my project." Becky grinned, showing all was forgiven.

It was as if Mia's brain had alerts set for any word, any discussion, that might in some way impact her. At the word *interview*, she appeared out of nowhere and joined their conversation in a flash. "Did you say 'interview'? Maybe I could be of help."

"Really? That would be amazing," Jade replied, shocking Zoe. "It's just for my journalism class, but I guess the school and local papers could pick it up if it's good enough."

"We can make it good enough," Mia said. Her confidence, while typically high, seemed to soar to an even loftier level. "You can interview me, and I can arrange for you to talk with Crispin." She glanced around the paddock expectantly, her eyes narrowing when Crispin was nowhere to be found. "It appears he needed to take Supersonic back to her stable, but I'm certain I'll be in touch with him soon."

"Thanks, Mia," Jade said.

Just as soon as she had invited herself into their conversation, Mia was off, hobnobbing with the other riders.

"Do you think it's a good idea to let Mia make your interview contacts for you?" Becky asked.

"Are you kidding? It would be great for my grade if I can talk to Crispin, and then I might even angle my way to talk to his dad," Jade replied, a sparkle in her eye. "Besides, I will do my fair share of research, but this is a good opportunity for me to get on the race grounds again."

Zoe had never seen Jade so pumped, not even at Junior Nationals. Her excitement about a school project only reminded Zoe about her complete lack of excitement for her own biology test that week. But she also remembered her promise to her mom about keeping schoolwork a top priority—she had to get home and study.

Later that week, following many late nights of studying and an intense exam on cell cycles, Zoe met Jade and Becky at Bright Fields for their lesson with Marcus. Every Friday, they had a group lesson on the flat, practicing their gaits and equitation. For Becky and Bob, who did dressage, many of the drills were a piece of cake—and they certainly added some extra flair to the lesson with

Raven

Me, Becky, and Jade

Raven and Me

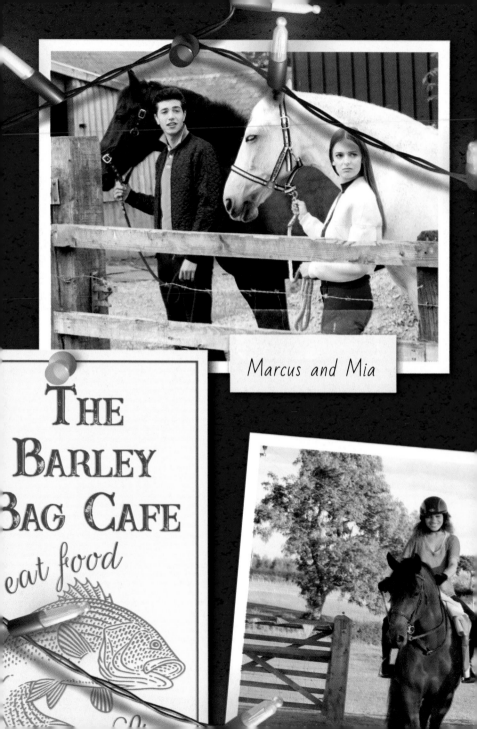

Marcus and Mia

THE BARLEY BAG CAFE
eat food

Rosie and Prince

Jade and Me

The Bright Fields gang

Pin and Me

Susie and Mia

THE ISLAND COUNTY SHOW

★ FUN FOR ALL THE FAMILY ★

AUGUST

BRIGHT FIELDS

their matching neon bandages, braided in Bob's mane and wrapped around Becky's leg.

As their lesson came to a close, Mia strode into the center of the ring as if she were modeling a formal gown during fashion week. "Yes, Mia?" Marcus asked. Mia waited for Jade, Becky, and Zoe to all congregate within hearing distance before she spoke.

"I just wanted to tell you that I will be missing my lessons for the next couple of weeks," Mia said solemnly.

"You don't want any more instruction leading up to the Classic?" Marcus asked, putting his hands in his vest.

"I don't think I'll gain much, going over these dinky fences again and again," Mia replied, motioning to the jumps that were set well over three feet and certainly not "dinky." "Not when I could practice over the actual obstacles, bushy hedgerows, and sparkling blue water pools." When no one responded immediately, she added, "As in, I'm going to Grindlerock to train with Crispin and Supersonic. That way, Firefly will be fully acclimated by the day of the race. I'm going on special invitation from Mr. Cooke himself. Marcus, I'll just need you to pack up a two-week supply of Firefly's feed so he won't colic from any changes in hay or grain." Mia turned with runway flair and walked right out of the ring without another word, leaving everyone behind her speechless.

"Mom, come on," Rosie insisted, holding open the door to the florist. A tiny silver bell jingled.

"Honestly, Rosie. Why aren't you at the stables with Zoe? I don't know why you're insisting on going to the flower shop." Her mother acted reluctant, but Rosie knew how much she loved flowers.

"Mom, I need your help. Mia has to have flowers for the day of the race, and I have no idea where to start." Rosie's voice was overflowing with anguish. She knew just how to get her mom invested.

"Why are Mia's flowers your responsibility?" her mom asked while leaning over to smell some pink blossoms with delicate petals.

"Honestly?" Rosie said. "Because no one else is going to do it, and it has to be done."

"Oh, they smell divine," her mom whispered emphatically, taking another long whiff of flower perfume. "Stock is one of my favorites." She took another sniff and moved on to some gorgeous blue delphiniums.

Rosie could tell she was hooked. "So, as you know, Bright Fields's colors are yellow and green," she said. "I've found Mia the perfect dress, and I hate to ruin its lines with a traditional corsage. So, the question is whether we do a wrist corsage *or* embellish her hat with some green-apple-hued flowers."

"Well, since you mention it, I might suggest apple blossoms," her mom said, raising her index finger like an antenna. "They are so sweet and dainty, but they're not seasonal. I think they really suggest spring rather than early autumn." She moved her hand to her chin, deep in thought. Rosie relished the moment. It was times like these that she knew where she got her attention to detail and her flair for pageantry.

"What about a chartreuse-green dahlia?" her mom declared as if it were a revelation. "They have such perfect architecture, so exquisite. And what about one in a bright accent color, like mango?"

"That would be way perfect," Rosie agreed. She kissed her fingertips to accentuate her point.

The mother-and-daughter duo was so caught up in their pursuit of the perfect flower combination that they didn't realize they were being watched. "Excuse me," a woman dressed all in black and white said. "Are you talking about the upcoming Grindlerock Classic?"

"Yes," Rosie answered uncertainly.

"Well," the woman said, adjusting the oversized cuffs of her pleated blouse. "I'm in charge of the luncheon and banquet preceding the big race. I'd love some consultation on how to bring some local appeal to the event, while still keeping it an exclusive, formal affair."

The woman was addressing Rosie's mother, but Rosie responded at once. "I understand," she said. "It must seem like a hefty task, but you have come to the right place. My mom grew up on the island, so she knows all of the establishments and their owners." Rosie flashed a smile in her mom's direction. "And I grew up in LA, so I can tell you which ones will deliver the upscale aura you desire."

The woman looked a bit surprised, then smiled. "I'm Aster," she said. "And you are fabulous." She put out her hand for an official shake. "How would you like to be our hostess on the big day?" she asked. "I would love to hire you on an hourly basis for your sage guidance as well."

Rosie considered the woman's pin-striped pencil skirt. Classic. Granted, her patent-leather heels were too high to wear on the ferry, let alone at an outdoor race-track, which made Rosie question her practical judgment. But she liked Aster's style. And Rosie could tell that Aster needed her.

"It's a deal," Rosie said.

Rosie let her mom and Aster work out the details. Now that she had a special role for the track's Opening Day ceremony, she decided it was only fitting to select some flowers for herself.

6

Zoe Phillips, (Sort of) Secret Agent

*B*ack at Bright Fields, the girls were still in shock about Mia's sudden departure. "This isn't good," Zoe said, shaking her head. "We let Mia down, and now she's going to train at the track with all the competition."

"At least she'll get to see the other horses and riders before the race," Becky pointed out. They were in the tack room, where they were supposed to be cleaning all the bits and bridles, which had not been done in months—possibly years.

"But wouldn't it be better if she'd stayed here, where there aren't as many distractions?" Zoe said, scratching the barn cat under its chin. "She's leaving the wise council of her girlfriends to hang out with a bunch of other super-competitive riders she doesn't even know. It doesn't seem right." She pulled the cat into a full-on cuddle.

"We are talking about Mia," Jade reminded Zoe. "She is very competitive. It could be just what she needs to prepare for the race."

"I just don't have a good feeling about it," Zoe admitted. "Aren't you worried about her, Jade? She got you several exclusive interviews for your article."

"She did," Jade admitted. "And she was very eloquent. I've used several of her quotes in what I've written so far."

Becky jumped in as soon as Jade paused. "But Mia made it clear that she wanted to be the biggest part of Jade's article."

"Come on," Zoe said. "We all know that Mia can be . . . all about herself. It's no surprise she wanted to be the star. But we are her stablemates, and we all look out for one another."

Just then, Susie entered the tack room, saddle in hand. It was clear from her expression that she'd overheard a good part of their conversation. "I'll admit," she said, hitching the saddle up on her hip, "I wasn't sure about her going there. But Mia seems very focused on the Classic. I'm pretty sure she's going because she thinks it's an opportunity to improve her chances in the race."

Zoe considered this. At one point, Zoe had thought of Susie as little more than Mia's doting minion, but Susie had proven she was loyal to all of Bright Fields's riders. Plus, she understood Mia better than anyone. Zoe supposed she shouldn't be so concerned about Mia. Maybe the truth was that she just felt bad that she hadn't been a better friend to Mia while she was training.

"I wouldn't worry," Susie said.

Zoe nodded, yet planned to try and convince Mia to stay one last time. But just then a sleek two-horse trailer pulled into the muddy Bright Fields drive. Despite all the pounding rain over the past several days, the trailer was shiny and spotless, as was the driver of the pickup pulling it. Crispin wore jeans, a navy rain slicker, and matching tall Hunter boots.

"He looks like he stepped right out of a riding catalog," Becky said.

"Yes, an expensive one," Jade added.

"Like the one that the Queen shops from," Susie confirmed. "She has top-notch taste when it comes to equestrian gear."

Zoe had to admit that Crispin certainly knew how to dress himself. She didn't even know the premier brands of riding attire. Mia, however, did.

On cue, Mia appeared, leading Firefly.

"Mia," Zoe said, rushing forward. "You don't have to go to Grindlerock."

"No, I don't have to," Mia agreed. "I *want* to go."

"You should stay. You'll be lonely there," Zoe insisted.

"That's silly. Daddy will be there with me, and there's Crispin and all the other riders," Mia said.

"You know what I mean," said Zoe. "We'll support you, Mia. I'm sorry we didn't help you train before."

Mia scoffed. "I didn't need your help. I just wanted the rest of you to feel included so you can feel like you're a part of my success when I win the Grindlerock Classic."

Zoe took a step back. That attitude was classic Mia. Either Mia was not in need of the council of her kindred horsewomen, or she was an Oscar-winning actress. Zoe sighed. "Well, you can feel free to come back. And if we don't see you before the race, we'll all be there, cheering you on," said Zoe, trying to sound as earnest as she could. When she glanced over at Becky, Jade, and Susie, they all smiled.

"Very well, then. Firefly and I will see you in the winner's circle," Mia said, tucking a single stray wisp of hair behind her ear. She gave them all a curt smile and loaded Firefly into the trailer.

All the while, Crispin had stood by the loading ramp not saying a word. After he closed the trailer ramp, he gave Mia a quick hug. "I'm so glad you're coming. All the other riders are way too serious."

Mia smiled and forced a laugh. "You know me," Mia said. "Not serious at all."

Zoe shook her head. Crispin had no idea what he was getting into!

"It'll be fun," he said to her. "They're almost done with all the fences, except the one my dad calls 'The Showstopper.' I'll be surprised if it's done by the race." He gave an easy laugh, and Zoe thought he might not be a bad guy after all. "Bye, everyone," he called to the other Bright Fields riders. "See you on Opening Day!"

Mia and Crispin got in the cab of the pickup. The truck and trailer pulled out of the drive, and life at Bright Fields returned to normal . . . except without Mia on the yard.

"I get everything Susie and Jade said," Zoe confided in Becky a little later. Jade had gone home for dinner with her parents. "But I still wish Mia had stayed at Bright

Fields up until race day. If she really wanted to, she could have taken Firefly over in a trailer the day before. But she's going to be there two whole weeks!"

Becky had her head tilted toward Zoe, eyes wide. "I know," she said. "Two whole weeks is a long time to resist the force of the Grindlerock Curse."

Zoe wasn't worried about a curse, but she was agreeing with Becky more and more that something wasn't quite right. Even putting aside those strange men with binoculars at the track—had Mr. Cooke invited all the Holloway riders to train at the track as well? If so, Holloway could be pretty underhanded when a competition was at stake. And, if not, why would Mr. Cooke single out Mia?

"Maybe we should try to check out Grindlerock for ourselves—and try to see *behind* that fence." Zoe gave Becky a knowing look. "Just to be sure."

"Hey, you two," Zoe's mom said, walking up behind them. "What are you plotting?"

"Mom, what are you doing here?" Zoe asked, trying to look casual.

"Rosie and I were just coming back from the pier. I brought you all some chocolate and biscuits," her mom explained. "Your sister did a tasting for the Race Day buffet."

"Well, that's a bonus of having an event planner for a sister," Zoe said, peeking in the bag full of sweets.

"But seriously," her mom said, "I get the idea that there is some drama in the works." She eyed both Zoe and Becky suspiciously. "We talked about this, Zoe. I don't want you chasing any more horse thieves or tracking down some lost treasure."

"That's exactly not what we did," said Becky, trying to defend herself.

"And that's not what we're doing, Mom," Zoe said, cutting Becky off before she went off on a tangent. "We were just planning a long trail ride, for fun." She looked at Becky, trying to get her to play along. "Why don't you come with us? We're going tomorrow."

"Oh, well, um, I don't know," Zoe's mom mumbled, clearly caught off guard.

"Come on, Mom. It's time you got back in the saddle again," Zoe said, nudging her with her elbow. Zoe was serious about her mom riding more, but that wasn't her only aim. She thought she could use the trail ride as a way to get a better look at what was happening on the Grindlerock grounds. And with her mom right there with them, how could she accuse the girls of being up to something?

"Oh, all right," her mom agreed good-naturedly. "Why not?"

Even though Zoe and her mom had invited Rosie to join them on the trail ride, Rosie had refused. "Ugh. It's been so rainy," she complained and then launched into a well-engineered excuse. "It's hard enough to keep Prince clean when we stay in the yard. I can't imagine all the mud and grit I'd have to scrub out of his fetlocks after the mucky trails. Besides, Marcus said he wants me to take another lesson, and I want to have all my energy for that."

Zoe thought Rosie was really missing out. It was the first clear day that they'd had on the island in a while. Zoe nearly lost herself in the peaceful calm of it all. The breeze was no more than a whisper.

Becky, however, was worried. She and Zoe had a plan—not only a plan, but also a secret code. It made her feel like a secret agent! It also made her nervous.

"I'm just concerned," Becky said as they were tacking up. "I really like your mum. I don't want to lie to her."

"You don't have to lie," Zoe assured her as she buckled Raven's bridle. "Remember, just disguise any information about Grindlerock as some kind of bird-watching comment. That way, I'll be able to get a sense of what you observe with your binoculars."

"And why aren't you wearing them?" Becky asked.

"Because if both of us had them, my mom would definitely know that something was up." Zoe smirked a little, feeling a bit like a secret agent herself.

"And what am I looking for?" Becky asked.

That was a good question. Zoe wasn't even sure. She still was just trusting her gut that something might not be right. "Just see if there's anything odd happening. Look for your ghouly ghost twins. And, of course, tell me if you see Mia."

"Very well. We'll do our best, won't we, Bob?" Becky said, giving Bob a pat.

The trail ride started innocently enough. The three horse-and-rider pairs cantered across the open meadow behind Bright Fields without saying much at all. "Mom, you look good," Zoe said, admiring her mother's easy way with her mount.

When they came to the end of the meadow, Zoe chose the path that would lead to Grindlerock, making sure it looked like a spontaneous decision. The passage was narrow, with lush trees and vines growing close to the trail. Here, where they had slowed to a walk, they chatted about a little bit of everything, which Zoe knew her mom appreciated.

It wasn't until they reached the steep hill that rose behind the Grindlerock grounds that Zoe's mom seemed to pick up on something strange happening. "Tell me, Becky, why do you have those field glasses with you again?" she asked, turning around in the saddle to make eye contact with her daughter's friend. She was on a lovely brown-and-white horse, Fletcher, one of Mia's rejects. Fletcher had a calm demeanor perfect for rides on the trails and the beach.

"Oh, these?" Becky asked, motioning to the binoculars strapped to her belt. She was trying her best to sound laid-back. "I've taken up bird-watching. I hear it's a good time of year to spot some, er, birds."

"How lovely," Zoe's mom said. "Are you into raptors or songbirds?"

"Oh, no, raptors are so scary! I prefer a sweet brontosaurus," Becky said cheerfully—then her eyes widened in horror as she realized Zoe's mom was talking about birds, not dinosaurs. "Uh, I mean . . ." She looked to Zoe, who was riding at the front, for guidance. Zoe gave a broad smile and a nod in an attempt to remind Becky to act natural. "I like the ones that, uh, fly?" Becky finally added.

"Got it," Zoe's mom said, looking skeptical.

"It's a new hobby, isn't it, Becky?" Zoe said pointedly, glancing back again.

"Yes," Becky agreed. "It's my newest."

"I wonder if there are any birds over there," Zoe prompted, looking down toward the racing grounds. Zoe could see horses on the course, but she couldn't focus on any details.

"Oh! I spot a *Firefly* falcon," Becky said, holding the binoculars to her eyes as Bob plodded on. "And a *Supersonic* sparrow! They both look really fast."

"Really?" Zoe said. "Do you know, Becky, are those two bird species particularly friendly?"

"Well, they are canter—" Becky caught herself. "I mean flying, wing to wing, as I speak," Becky finished, eyes still glued to the binocular lenses.

"Okay, that's enough," Zoe's mom said, pulling up Fletcher and first staring down Becky and then all-out glaring at Zoe. "What's going on here?"

Zoe bit her lip. She knew her mom wanted her to limit the drama. How many times had she been warned to keep out of other people's business? There was only one thing worse than telling her mom the truth, and that would be hearing Becky come up with an outlandish explanation of the afternoon's shenanigans.

"Mom, don't get mad," Zoe began. She paused and tried to think of the perfect white lie. She could feel her whole face tense up as she looked her mom in the eye. So much for being secret agents. "Please don't get mad," she blurted, "but we're spying on Mia."

Pony Squad Sleuthing

W ell, your mom took that so much better than I thought she would," Becky said when she and Zoe reconvened later that day. "I wholeheartedly believed she was going to make me hand over my binoculars and never give them back. And maybe even call my parents."

"Totally," Zoe agreed. Her mom seemed young and hip, but she could be quite the disciplinarian as well. "She's been making a big deal about me minding my own business lately, making good decisions, avoiding conflict. I wasn't sure how she would take the truth."

Zoe's mom had actually laughed off their confession. She told Zoe that it was good to look out for her friends—but also that she and Becky were probably overreacting, and that Mia was just fine training at Grindlerock. True, Zoe hadn't exactly shared the whole story. She hadn't told her mom about the creepy water fence obstacle on the track, the men with binoculars Becky had seen, or the potential for sabotage from Holloway. Zoe had a feeling those details would make her mom find the whole thing much less amusing.

"Okay, so now that my mom isn't listening in, tell me what you saw yesterday," she prompted Becky.

"Well, I did spot a yellow-browed warbler, which is extremely rare in these parts," Becky said.

"Wait, what? Are you talking about a bird?" Zoe asked.

"Yes," Becky confirmed. "It had the loveliest olive-green plumage on its underbelly." Becky flashed Zoe a winning smile. "I've been practicing that all afternoon. But seriously, I'm sure that I saw a warbler. I read that it's a big deal for bird people!"

"Becky," Zoe said, her tone serious. "I'm asking what you saw on the *course*, with Mia."

"Oh, yes, right. I saw Firefly and Supersonic galloping along the track. Mia and Crispin seemed to be training together, in perfect sync. There were also four other horses, none of which looked to be from Holloway. Two bays, a liver chestnut, and a dapple gray," Becky said, sounding very matter-of-fact in her explanation. Perhaps she would make a good secret agent after all. "From where we were, I could see from the starting point, along the straight stretch of hedgerow hurdles, and around the bend to some of the cross-country fences." She took a breath. "With the binoculars really focused, I could make out all the way to the water fence in the gully. It looked totally flooded. There was a mini earthmover and at least two men with shovels, working on it."

"There has been a lot of rain recently," Zoe commented, thinking about how the water could easily collect in the gully. "Was one of the men working there Liam? We could ask him what happened."

"It was pretty far away," Becky said. "But I don't think he was there."

"Well, it doesn't sound all that suspicious, just like bad timing for a storm," Zoe had to admit. So why did she still feel like something wasn't right? "I just wish we could get onto the grounds."

"Have you seen the security at that place?" Becky pointed out. "It's like they think the muck buckets are encrusted with the crown jewels."

"Why don't you come with me?" said a voice.

Zoe let out a scream in surprise. "Jade! Why are you creeping up on us?"

"Um, I'm not. You are in a totally public part of the stables, which are also public," Jade pointed out. "I am in no way creeping."

"Sorry," Zoe said. "We're just talking about Grindlerock."

"I know a way to get you in," Jade suggested. "But you'd have to go undercover. I need someone to help me take photographs for my article."

"Totally," Zoe said. "I can bring my mom's camera."

"What about me?" Becky asked. "Can I come, too?"

"Of course," Jade said.

"What is my job?" Becky asked eagerly. "If Zoe is the photographer, what am I?"

Jade looked uncertain, but it was clear she knew she needed to give Becky an important-sounding job, too. "You know what?" Jade said, buying time. "I need a second set of eyes. I'm essentially reporting on the obvious, the grand reopening, but I need someone to be looking for the behind-the-scenes, nitty-gritty story that not everyone suspects." Jade paused and looked to Zoe to see if she had successfully sold the idea.

Standing behind Becky, Zoe gave a big thumbs-up.

"What do you think, Becky?" Jade asked. "Would you be interested?"

They nearly needed to scrape Becky's jaw off the sawdust-covered floor. "Um, *yeah*, I'd be interested," Becky replied. "That's, like, just the kind of thing I can do!"

"Great. We can head over after school tomorrow," Jade said. "And"—she hesitated—"since there's a chance I can talk to Mr. Cooke, could you both try to look a little professional?"

"Absolutely," Becky said.

"So," Jade said, narrowing her eyes at Becky. "What is something you might not wear, if you were going to look professional? I ask only because you are my dearest, best friend, and I know your wardrobe so well."

Becky bit her lip and drew in a deep breath. Zoe suspected she was attempting to visualize her closet, her dresser drawers, and even the clothes that were currently in the laundry bin. "After deep consideration," Becky began, "I'll go with 'no homemade tie-dye T-shirts or bedazzled pink chaps'?"

"Yes," Jade said. "That was the right answer for two thousand points. Thanks, Becky."

Becky did not forget her promise to Jade. Zoe barely recognized her. Becky had on a short, fitted tweed jacket with tailored trousers and brown Chelsea boots. Her hair was pulled up into two twisty buns. "I had to get Mum to help," Becky admitted. "I can only do braids."

"Gosh, Becky," Jade said. "You look super. Thanks for taking this seriously."

"I feel underdressed," Zoe declared. "And I actually wore a skirt!" Her denim-skirt-and-cardigan outfit had inspired comments from both her mom and Rosie that morning. Zoe did not often attempt to dress up.

"You both look great," Jade said. "Thank you so much."

Jade's dad picked them up in front of the school and dropped them off at Grindlerock. "I'll be back after I run all the errands on your mum's list," he said to Jade, waving a long strip of paper in his hand. "Which could take a while . . ."

"Okay, Dad," Jade said. She waved good-bye and then pulled out her phone. "Liam said he'll let us in, and then it's up to us to find people to talk to and get some good photographs."

"So you don't have any specific interviews scheduled?" Becky asked.

"Nope, we're winging it," Jade said, sounding proud of

herself for moving forward without a minute-by-minute agenda. "You can take bets on how long it will take for them to kick us out."

"They won't kick us out," Zoe said with confidence. "You're giving them free publicity."

"We'll see," Jade replied, sounding rather upbeat. "Mr. Cooke was super helpful last week, but when I called about coming back for a follow-up, he was rather rude. He was like a totally different person."

"So, you think they might be hiding something here after all?" Becky suggested. "Like the truth about the curse. That's why you need me."

"Exactly," Jade responded without a beat, but Zoe could tell that Jade was just humoring her best friend. Despite what she had said about the management of the track, Jade didn't seem concerned. She tucked her blouse in so it was smooth under her jacket, took a deep breath, and put her shoulders back. Jade was ready for business!

When Liam opened the heavy, ornate gate, he did not seem upbeat. He greeted them politely, but he looked exhausted.

"We've been working nonstop. The downpours have absolutely saturated the track, which is a bigger concern on the cross-country fences," he said. "We don't want horses skidding out. We have shipments of sand, soil stabilizer, and new turf coming in."

Becky's eyes glazed over at more talk of soil.

"Maybe you'll get paid overtime?" Jade said hopefully. "It sounds like a lot of work."

"It is. Plus, they still have us altering some of the fences," Liam added. He pulled a large stainless-steel water bottle from his bag and took a long, steady swig.

"Yeah," Zoe spoke up, seeing her opening. "We went on a trail ride up the ridge behind Grindlerock two days ago, and Becky noticed that the one water fence in the gully was totally flooded out."

"That one is a mess. I'm not sure why, but it's so bad that they called in special outside contractors to fix it," Liam explained. "That way, us regular crew members can focus on all the other trouble points. Even with the contractors, the water fence isn't supposed to be ready until Opening Day. Someone said that the boss has started calling it 'The Showstopper.'"

Zoe remembered that Crispin had mentioned that name, too. So that strange water fence was also the big "showstopper." That couldn't be a coincidence.

"Do you think the track will be ready?" Jade asked. "It's coming up so soon!"

"Off the record?" Liam asked, eyeing Jade's notepad and pen.

"Yes, off the record," Jade responded with a smile. "As friends."

"I think it'll be tight, but I'm pretty sure we'll make it. We're only responsible for the track and the fences," Liam explained, adjusting his ball cap. "They have some ritzy firm coming in to do the plants and flowers for the Race Day Banquet. It's going to be top-notch."

Zoe swallowed a chuckle. She couldn't help it. What would Liam say if he knew her ten-year-old sister was a consultant for the ritzy decoration firm? Not only that, Rosie had also been practicing her Race Day Banquet speech for days. Zoe could hear her practicing from her bedroom. Rosie's voice carried so well it could practically pierce noise-canceling headphones. Zoe could hear her rattle off the Grindlerock sponsors and the names of the horses and riders again and again, each time with a different inflection, as she fell asleep.

"Well, since I let you in, I hope you don't get into too much trouble," Liam said.

"We'll be careful," Jade assured him.

"We promise," said Zoe. She had wondered before if Liam might be in on whatever weirdness was going on at Grindlerock, but she didn't feel that way anymore. He was letting them in to look around, after all. He just wanted to do his job and do it well.

"Okay, have fun," Liam said.

"Let's just hope we don't step into a quicksand trap," Becky added, eyes darting around suspiciously.

Liam laughed until he saw that Becky's expression was deadly serious. "Well, uh, text me if you need me," Liam advised, giving Becky a strange look. "Otherwise, I'll be knee-deep in the muck, so to speak."

"Good luck," Jade said. Zoe and Becky offered their well wishes, too. Then the three girls headed toward the stable block. As they strolled around the track grounds, the Bright Fields riders appreciated the classic details of the old buildings. They were also impressed with the obvious upgrades. "It's very tidy," Becky commented.

"The main stable block is over this way." Jade pointed. "It's where Supersonic and Firefly are boarded."

Jade headed in that direction, walking with purpose and acting like she had every right to be there. But as soon as they turned down the main aisle of the barn, she jumped and yanked Becky and Zoe into a nearby office, out of sight. "That was Mr. Cooke," Jade said, looking sheepish. The sharp-dressed race promoter had been talking to a man they didn't know just a few feet away!

"So? I thought you wanted to talk to him," Zoe said.

"I do," Jade said. "But when I saw him again, it just reminded me how gruff he was over the phone when I asked to come back. I feel like he's not going to talk to me." With her back flat against the door, she cautiously peeked into the aisle. "Let's just get a few photos and go."

Zoe knelt down. She stuck the viewfinder of her mom's camera right in the crack, where the door was ajar, and started taking pictures.

"He's talking to a vet," Jade whispered.

"How do you know that?" asked Becky.

"Deductive reasoning skills," said Jade. "And also the fact that his jacket has VET embroidered on the left side. But I didn't mean photograph *them*, Zoe," she added.

"Why not?" Zoe whispered back. "Might as well photograph as much as we can while we're here."

Meanwhile, Becky had started to look around the room. "And what are *you* doing?" Jade asked.

"Just what you told me to," Becky said, carefully sorting through papers on a desk. "I'm looking for the untold story." Becky still wanted to answer some of her many lingering questions about the place. "Like, see here, why are there lots of diagrams of one fence here, but none of the others? Didn't Liam say they were updating all the fences?"

"Is it a water fence?" Jade asked.

"Yes," Becky answered, sounding surprised.

"Didn't you hear that they have special people working on one of the water fences?" Jade questioned. "That must be why there are only plans for the one fence here. The plans for all the other fences are probably somewhere else."

"Very well," Becky replied and placed the paper back down on the desk. Next, she took out her phone.

"Wait! Why are you taking pictures of it?" Jade whispered again.

"Because Zoe is busy taking pictures over there, and this might be important."

Jade sighed, but returned her attention to Mr. Cooke and the vet.

"They're talking a long time," she said, sneaking a look out the door.

"Yes, and Mr. Cooke just paid the vet," said Zoe, "in cash."

"Well, vets are paid for their services," Jade said. "I don't think that's really relevant to my article."

"It was one of those fat bundles of cash, all rolled up

and rubber-banded," Zoe said. "That's weird, right? What is he, a mobster?"

"Do you subscribe to the same cable mystery channel as Becky?" Jade teased. "I'm starting to question why I invited you in the first place."

"Because," Becky chirped, "despite all your brilliant scientific reasoning and precise calculations, you can't aim a camera."

"Oh, right," Jade said with consideration. "I am getting better, though."

"Oh, shoot. He's coming this way," Zoe said. Instinctively, she shoved Jade to the back corner of the room. "Quick, get under here." She threw a very hairy horse blanket over them. "Becky, under the desk! Hurry!"

Zoe and Jade could hear Becky scramble. And then, the only sounds were footsteps and a very off-key whistle.

Zoe peeked out and could see the vet, who had a particularly unfortunate dye job, remove his white lab coat and put on another jacket before leaving the office. The girls waited a full minute before emerging from their hiding spots, just in case he doubled back for something.

"Whoa, that was close," Jade said, throwing the smelly blanket off her head. "Not that we were really doing anything wrong. But I don't want to get Liam in trouble for letting us in."

"I don't know if that vet is really a vet," Becky blurted out. "I could see from under the desk. It was the same guy who had binoculars that day that we came for the track tour. Well, one of them, anyway. Who knows where his ghost twin is."

"No," Zoe said. "That doesn't make sense."

"I'm pretty sure," Becky said. "Like 98.7536 percent sure. He had that same horrid dye job. It had to be the same guy, so I'm just going to say it. The so-called vet and Mr. Cooke are up to something."

"I'm with Zoe," Jade said. "And the other 1.2464 percent of you. That doesn't make sense."

"Good math," Becky said.

"What do you think?" Zoe asked. "How crazy is it to still try to get some pictures?"

They agreed to do another quick loop around the grounds before calling it a day. When they left the office they nearly ran right into Mia—who looked on the verge of tears until she saw Zoe, Jade, and Becky. She sniffed and lifted her chin. "I don't know why you three aren't racing. You're all so interested in this place, you might as well."

"I was just finishing up my article," Jade said in a hushed voice, hoping not to attract too much attention. "I just need photos. We won't be long."

"Well, I'd offer up Firefly, because the cameras just love him," Mia began. Before she could say more, her voice broke. "But he won't be racing this weekend, so what's the point?" she said, rushing through the sentence, her words jumbled with emotion. Mia's chin quivered, but she sniffed again and forced herself to regain composure. A single tear started to run down her cheek. She quickly wiped it away as she shared the sad news that Firefly was injured.

All three of her Bright Fields stablemates offered her sincere apologies, and Mia seemed to take some comfort in that.

"It's a rare tendon condition," Mia said. "I'm lucky the vet recognized it."

The three friends exchanged looks at the mention of a vet, but said nothing.

Zoe finally broke the silence. "That's horrible. Will he be all right?"

Mia nodded, her lips pursed. "It just requires rest and he'll make a full recovery."

"That's good news," Jade said.

"I suppose so," Mia replied. "We were doing so well in practice. I think we really had a shot. I thought it would be good for Daddy's business prospects with Mr. Cooke, if I could win." She sighed. "But most of all, I really wanted it for Firefly and me. I wanted to prove we could do it. We always seem to come in second place." Her voice faded at the end, and she stared at her high boots, caked with mud.

Becky, Jade, and Zoe exchanged glances, unsure how to comfort Mia. Zoe wondered if Mia was actually referring to their placement at Junior Nationals, or if she felt like she had finished second place in some other way. Mia was certainly the top rider at Bright Fields, but she always seemed to need something more.

Mia sniffed again, her eyes still lowered.

"You and Firefly had a shot," Becky said tentatively.

"You totally did." Zoe reached out and placed a comforting hand on Mia's shoulder, and Mia did not flinch away.

8

The Plot Thickens

After she had regained her composure, Mia ushered the three girls around the grounds, pointing out areas of interest for photos. She started, not surprisingly, at Firefly's stall. The thoroughbred looked as gallant as always, except his front left leg was encased in a thick pillow wrap. "He's a little groggy from the medication," Mia said, stroking the horse's neck. She stood under his head and faced his chest, giving him a long hug. "You'll get better soon, boy, and then we'll show them," she whispered loud enough that they all could hear. Zoe wasn't sure she had seen Mia that affectionate toward Firefly since they had been reunited after his horse-napping. He seemed to enjoy it.

Next, Mia showed them around the stables. Jade seemed less skittish, now that Mia was with them. Mia walked down the aisles and through the yard much like she did at Bright Fields—as if she owned the place.

"What's this?" Zoe asked when they came to a building that was almost entirely glass. Its roof was rounded and looked like a well-cut gem, the panels of tinted glass spiraling together to a point.

"It was originally a greenhouse," Mia explained, "but it's been renovated to be the jockey lounge." She held the door open for the three girls and waited for their reaction.

"Are you kidding me?" Becky said, running up to a classic pinball machine. "It's like a vintage arcade."

"They have a Sub-Zero fridge," Zoe added longingly, feeling her stomach churn with hunger.

"And they have two bathrooms?" Jade commented in disbelief. "With showers?"

"It's quite nice," Mia agreed, "but it's been empty practically all week. Not nearly as lively as the hay bales back at Bright Fields. Though it's certainly cleaner."

Zoe examined Mia's expression. Was Mia actually feeling nostalgic for the stables, still being rebuilt after the summer fire? Zoe loved Bright Fields, but she imagined

Mia would feel more at home at a place with all these amenities.

At Jade's prompting, Zoe pointed the camera everywhere they went. She took as many angles and exposures as she could: the hedgerow hurdles, the turn-out fields, the homestretch, the special box seats at the finish line. Eventually, the light started to fade, and Jade got a text that her dad had finished with his errands and was waiting for them.

"Thanks so much, Mia," Jade said. "That was really helpful."

"I don't suppose I have much else to do," Mia said wistfully. "After all, I can't exactly train without a horse."

"Will you be coming back to Bright Fields early, then?" Zoe asked. "We miss you on the yard."

Mia sighed. "Probably not," she said. "Everyone is so busy around here, especially now that the race is so close. I'm not even sure I could get anyone to trailer Firefly back for me."

"I'm sure Marcus would come to get you," Zoe commented. "It isn't that far."

"We'll see," Mia said, but she didn't sound in a hurry to return to life as usual.

The next day, when Zoe saw Susie at Bright Fields, she considered the best way to tell her about Firefly. But it soon became clear that Mia had already told her. In fact, Susie had an even more recent update.

"Mia was still worried about Firefly, obviously," Susie explained, "but she's still going to compete in the Classic."

"What? How?" Zoe asked. "I thought the vet said Firefly needs rest in order for his tendon to heal."

"That's the thing," Susie said. "She isn't riding Firefly. She's riding Supersonic."

"Supersonic?!" Becky and Jade exclaimed at once when Zoe tracked them down in the tack room to share the latest.

"Supersonic," Zoe confirmed. "That's what she told Susie, at least."

"But what about Crispin?" Jade wondered. "I thought Mr. Cooke had said that Crispin was riding his horse."

"No idea," Zoe replied. "Maybe Mia sweet-talked him into giving up his chance to race for her." She was only half joking—she wouldn't put it past Mia.

"Come to think of it," Jade said, not listening to Zoe, "I asked Mia if we could get a picture of Crispin when we were there yesterday, but she said she hadn't seen him in a couple of days. She had been so keen on training that she claims she hadn't really noticed."

"Maybe he had to go back to the mainland for school?" Jade suggested, thinking practically.

"Maybe," Zoe said.

"Or maybe the Grindlerock Curse finally scared him away," Becky offered, but Zoe noticed that she didn't say it with much conviction.

The three friends sat on the tack trunks, all befuddled.

"Does it really matter?" Jade said finally. "Mia will still get to ride."

"Yeah," Zoe agreed. "It's not as if it will affect your article in any way, right?"

"It shouldn't. I turned in my first draft today. We'll get it back and need to do revisions by tomorrow to make the paper."

"Your teacher sounds intense," Zoe said, feeling a little relieved that she hadn't chosen journalism as one of her electives.

"So, if Jade is practically done with her article and Mia still gets to race, we don't care anymore that there seem to be a number of peculiar happenings?" Becky asked, looking pointedly at her friends. "And I'm not talking about a curse this time, I swear."

"Then what?" Jade asked.

"Well, there was Mr. Cooke paying the vet with a roll of bills," Becky suggested.

"Someone had to pay him for helping Firefly," Jade pointed out.

"Yes, but why would Mr. Cooke pay? Why not Mia's dad? And why cash for something so expensive?" Becky's eyebrows were raised so high it seemed that they might fly right off her forehead.

"True," Zoe said. "We all know you can't exactly pay for a vet visit with the five-dollar bill in your back pocket."

"These are all good questions," Jade said, "but they don't add up to a crime or anything." Jade carefully folded a set of rags, all freshly laundered, that she had brought back from home.

"So, now that your article is done, you are perfectly fine with whatever is going down?" Becky probed.

"Well, yes, because now I have an AP Chemistry test to study for, so I checked the article off my list, literally, and I need to move on," Jade explained.

"What about the men with binoculars on the ridge?" Becky prompted.

"We have already discussed the fact that they could easily have been there to observe how the horses handled the track," Jade replied.

"Don't you think it's odd that that is the very fence that is under reconstruction by an outside firm?" Becky questioned further.

"That fence was always different, though," Zoe said, "the way it's between those two hills. They could have hired a special firm because of that."

"It's just such a stretch, trying to connect all these facts," Jade said, creasing the folds of her final rag.

Becky had worked herself up. She ripped the hair out of one of Bob's brushes and tossed it to the ground. Zoe knew that Becky would eventually pick up the hair and throw it in the muck pile, but she could tell her friend needed to vent a little. Becky smoldered in the silence—at least until there was a buzz of a cell phone.

Jade looked sheepish. "That's mine," she said, shifting to pull her phone out of her backpack. "It's Liam." She looked surprised to see his name.

"If Liam, with all his landscape know-how and peat prowess, said something was going on, you'd listen to him," Becky insisted, but Jade didn't react. She just scowled at her phone, reading a text.

"He's asking me if our friend is really riding Supersonic in the Classic," Jade said. "Why would he care? He hasn't mentioned any of the horses or the riders before."

"Well, it is getting closer to the race. Maybe now that all his hard work on the track is almost done, he can start thinking about the fun stuff," Zoe said with a shrug. "Uh, not that the soil stuff isn't totally fun, too," she added quickly for Jade's benefit.

"He's calling," Jade said, quickly tapping her phone and putting it to her ear.

Zoe and Becky listened to her side of the conversation, but it didn't reveal anything. When Jade hung up, she looked confused. "Have either of you heard of Monty's pet python?"

Now Becky and Zoe looked confused, too. "Who in the world is Monty and why does he have a python as a pet?" Zoe asked.

"Yeah, personally, I'd go with a pet bunny myself," Becky added. "Or a guinea pig—so fluffy."

"What does this Monty guy have to do with anything?" Zoe asked.

"I'm not entirely sure," Jade said. "Liam was talking under his breath, but he said he overheard some grooms talking about the race. One of them told the other guy that he had to watch the race. That something big was going to happen to Supersonic," she continued. "That the boss had already taken care of Firefly. And that it was all part of the boss's big plan for Monty's pet python."

"Wait, Liam said this?" Zoe asked.

"Yes," Jade confirmed. "At least, it's what he overheard."

"Well, I was right," Becky said, closing her trunk. "Now that Liam thinks something weird is happening, you're on board."

"Well, this adds a whole new level to things, doesn't it?" Jade said. "This is the first time snakes have come into the mix! And I'm assuming this boss they keep referring to is Mr. Cooke, right? Who else would it be?"

"I'm confused," Zoe said. "Mr. Cooke would never do anything to ruin Supersonic's chances. It's his horse." She paused. "If anything, he'd try to get rid of Supersonic's prime competition." Then the reality of it set in. "Wait, you don't think that Mr. Cooke would do something on purpose to take Firefly out of the competition, do you? That groom said something about 'taking care of Firefly.'"

"Like what? Pay off a vet with a big roll of money?" Becky suggested.

"Exactly like that, Becky," Jade admitted. "Exactly like that."

After a little Internet research, the girls figured out that Firefly had been the local favorite to win the Grindlerock Classic. "It looks like someone had posted footage of Mia practicing at the track, so people must have been excited about his chances," Zoe told the others.

"If you come in first, you get that huge winner's purse," Jade reminded them. "So with Firefly not racing, Supersonic is the new favorite."

"So Mr. Cooke will win all that money," Becky said.

"In theory," Zoe replied, looking at her phone, "but this website says that Mr. Cooke is only a part owner. Supersonic actually belongs to a whole group of friends who bought her as a business investment, so they probably would split the prize money."

"But I still don't understand how this guy Monty fits

into it all," Becky said. "Is Monty one of the owners? Is he going to bring his pet python to the race?" She cringed at the thought. "And why would Liam tell you about this, Jade? Was he trying to get you to warn Mia about something?"

"I don't know. His voice was so muffled it was hard to make out some of what he said," Jade said miserably. "Why would he call me? What could I possibly do?"

"Well," Becky began, "he probably realizes the power of Pony Squad. And, while he might not think you could do anything on your own, as just one person, he knows we've always got your back and we can help." Becky looked to Zoe.

"Exactly!" Zoe said. "Liam is trusting us to make heads or tails of what he overheard, so I think Pony Squad needs to come up with a plan."

9

Puzzling Problems

Unfortunately, it was far easier to declare the awesome power of Pony Squad than to actually devise an awesome plan. They only had two days before the race, and they didn't have much more than a few hunches. "We need more information. And proof," Zoe insisted. "Otherwise, no one will listen to us."

"Do we have any incriminating evidence?" Jade asked.

Zoe went through all the dubious situations in her head. There were a lot of them—the vet, Firefly's injury, Mia's reassignment to ride Supersonic, Crispin's unexplained disappearance, the grooms' comments about Monty, the men in suits with binoculars. Becky had a hard time admitting it, but there wasn't anything concrete.

Still pacing, Jade shook her head. "It's just a complicated puzzle with pieces that don't quite fit."

"Yes, but when you look at the big picture, the image on the cover of the puzzle box is money, money, money," Becky said triumphantly. Her friends looked at her, confused. "You know, the cover of the box always shows what the puzzle is about?"

Zoe's eyes lit up. "No, you're right!"

"I am?"

"Yes!" Zoe said. "The whole reason Mr. Cooke is reopening the racetrack is to make money. It's a business investment, so it's not a bad idea to think about money. It's a big motivator, right? I mean, money was the whole reason Sam had Raven kidnapped."

Zoe's statement silenced Becky and Jade for a moment. Sam had been Bright Fields's owner when Zoe first came to the island from LA. Becky and Jade had both known Sam for a long time. She had been their trainer and friend. Even though Sam had been trying to save Bright Fields from bankruptcy, she had betrayed all the riders at the stables by putting their horses in danger, and she had broken the law. Sometimes people do the wrong thing for the right reasons— but it was not an easy lesson for any of them to learn.

"It's been a long day," Jade said with a sigh. "Maybe we should go home and focus on something fun, like homework!"

"Ha ha," said Zoe sarcastically.

"You just want to study for your AP Chemistry test," Becky teased Jade.

"Well, it is a very important test," Jade said.

Zoe was distracted the rest of the night. How was Jade able to focus on studying? Zoe returned to what Jade had said. They needed more information. She thought about the few sources that they had. She pulled out her camera and scrolled through the saved photos from Grindlerock.

Jade had made her take pictures of all the stalls, all the horses, the building equipment, a worker in a suit carrying a big bag of dirt, even a fancy water trough. Zoe scrolled back and looked at the shot of the worker in the suit. Sure enough, it was the man with the unattractive yellow hair. Now he was carrying sand? What didn't he do at the racecourse?

Next, Zoe scrolled to a picture of Mia with Firefly. Zoe hadn't seen Mia since that day. Mia was riding the race favorite, Supersonic. If anyone had new information, it would be her.

Zoe pushed her biology book to the back of her desk and pulled out her phone. She and Mia didn't exactly have a late-night texting habit, but it was worth a try.

Zoe> Hey, Mia. Just saying hey. Heard you're riding Supersonic. Crazy!! :O

Mia> Not that crazy. Mr. Cooke needed a rider so he asked me.

Zoe was relieved that Mia sounded a little more like herself again.

Zoe> You weren't surprised?

Mia> Not surprised someone wanted to take advantage of my availability, especially since I have so much experience on the renovated track. Plus MC said he'd had his eye on me for a while. So flattering. Of course I'd ride for the promoter of the track! And Supersonic is such a star. She's a blast to ride.

Zoe> How's Firefly?

Mia On the mend. He's in such good spirits you wouldn't even suspect he was injured. ☺

Zoe Do you think you have a chance? How is Supersonic compared to other horses in training?

Zoe knew it was a long shot. Mia was far too proud to reveal if she was having any problems riding Supersonic. But if Liam was right, Mr. Cooke apparently thought there was another horse at Grindlerock who could easily beat them.

Mia Supersonic is the best.

Zoe Any word from Crispin?

Mia Yes! He's coming back for Opening Day. And he told me he has some special race day advice for how to handle the track with Supersonic. So sweet.

Zoe Special advice? Like what?

Mia Something about how I shouldn't take a tight turn on some fence, which makes no

sense. At all. I'll take the tightest turns possible because I intend to win.

Zoe You go! ☺

Sometimes, Zoe really admired Mia's confidence. (Or
was it stubbornness?) But was it wise to brush off Crispin's
advice? Was he really trying to help her, or was he trying
to help his father sabotage her chances at winning?

Mia I can keep up with the front-runners. I'm not
afraid to fight for the rail.

Zoe Why isn't Crispin riding?

Mia Zoe! What's with all the questions!?! My
thumbs are wearing out, and I need them in
prime shape for Saturday!

Ugh! Zoe couldn't believe it. She hadn't gotten anywhere. It was like Zoe had found a whole new pocketful
of puzzle pieces that didn't fit with one another—or the
big picture. It was a mess.

As Zoe was getting ready for bed, she overheard Rosie

practicing her announcements for the Race Day Banquet. Zoe didn't know how Rosie did it, but her sister hardly needed any sleep. She knocked on her door and peeked her head in.

"Hey, just saying good night," Zoe said.

"Good night," Rosie replied.

"Don't you think you've practiced enough?" Zoe asked.

"You'd think so, but Aster keeps sending me different versions. There are new horses, different riders. Look at all these!" Rosie slapped a thick stack of papers on her desk. "I've been practicing my accents for all the foreign jockeys."

Zoe's eyes skimmed the paper on top of the stack as Rosie spoke. Halfway down the page, she saw something that made her heart jump in her chest.

"Does that say Monty's Pet Python?" she asked, trying to keep her voice casual.

"Blech! Yes!" Rosie replied. "What an awful name, right? No matter how I say it, it really messes with the whole flow of my introduction."

"Fascinating," Zoe said under her breath. So there was no man named Monty and no actual python—Monty's Pet Python was a horse! "What about Firefly? Is he still listed in the current script? Or have they taken him off?"

At first, Rosie gave her sister a blank stare. "I kind of just read the names and don't really think about it, or else I lose my rhythm. But I don't think Firefly was ever listed."

"Where's the first script?" Zoe demanded.

Rosie looked at her sister as if she were the special kind of crazy that belonged on a reality TV show. "It's at the bottom of the pile," Rosie responded. "They're chronological." How was it that Rosie left dozens of fingernail polish bottles all over the house, but she had the banquet scripts in chronological order?

Zoe grabbed the stack and ripped out the bottom sheet. She scanned the lengthy opening and then went through the list of names. "Sheesh! You have to read all of these? I hope they're paying you because—" But then Zoe stopped short of finishing. "You're sure this was the first one?"

"The date is at the top," Rosie said.

"It's from almost two weeks ago," Zoe said.

"Yeah," Rosie confirmed. "Aster sent it the day after we met at the flower shop, along with my contract. She was anxious for me to commit."

"But this has Mia riding Supersonic from the start," Zoe said, her brain taking the puzzle piece and trying to fit it in place. "Even before Firefly was hurt."

"The Firefly thing was pretty tragic, huh?" Rosie said. "Mia and I had to scrap her whole Bright Fields yellow-and-green picnic ensemble and switch to something using Grindlerock's color palette. We ended up with a lavender A-line number. It's clean and classy, but it lacks the vibrancy of the original outfit." Rosie's tone had an air of nostalgia. "Anyway, can I have my script back?" she asked, holding out her hand.

"I don't suppose I could keep this one?" Zoe asked. "It's old anyway."

Rosie huffed. "Fine. The only script I really care about is the one on top. I'm trying to memorize the salutation now. I just hope I don't get any more updates from Aster, because I haven't even finalized my outfit for the big day."

"You'll have to be sure to make time for that," Zoe agreed.

"And you know you aren't leaving the house on Saturday until you get my approval, right?"

"I'm counting on it," Zoe replied, trying to humor her sister in hopes of escaping soon. "But I am certain my outfit won't rival yours."

"Well, obviously, because Mr. Cooke invited me to sit in the box seats with him, right at the finish line, so you know I'm going to bring it in the fashion department."

Zoe gulped. "You're sitting with Mr. Cooke?"

"Of course," Rosie replied, putting one hand on her hip, her nails now lavender with fuchsia hearts. "After all, I am the hostess of the whole event."

"Of course," Zoe said, trying to sound proud of her little sister's prime role in the day's festivities. But now she had one more person to worry about on Opening Day.

After school, Zoe, Jade, and Becky headed to the stables together. They discussed all the oddities discovered in Rosie's scripts, including the revelation about Monty's Pet Python.

"So it's true, or it might be true, that Mr. Cooke has a secret entry into the race that he's keeping under the radar with the plan of winning big," Zoe said, hoping that talking it through would make everything sound a little less crazy. It didn't.

"But we still won't have any hard evidence until we see if Monty's Pet Python actually wins tomorrow," Jade said. "And it isn't a crime for him to have another entry in the race. We'd have to prove that he played a part in Firefly's injury or something else illegal."

Zoe felt like her mind might explode, and she still had to get ready for a lesson with Marcus! She was not surprised when she couldn't focus on the jumping courses that afternoon any better than she had been able to focus on her school courses the night before. "Where is your head, Zoe?" Marcus said. "Or, forget about your head, your whole body is somewhere else. Your hands are sloppy, you're flopping all over the place, you can't find his rhythm to save your life." Marcus took a deep breath and shook his head. "I'm sorry to be so hard on you, but I'm a bit worried. Raven is chomping at the bit, ready for the races, and you look like you wouldn't make it through a leisurely beach ride."

Zoe stared at Marcus. He could really dish out the brutal honesty.

The worst part was that Marcus was right. Raven was pawing at the ground, snorting, and prancing on the spot. He wanted to tackle the jumps that Marcus had set up in the ring. All week, Zoe had been caught up in the Grindlerock drama, and she'd hardly paid attention to Raven at all.

"I can't do this," Zoe said abruptly. "I can't ride today." Zoe threw her leg over the saddle and dismounted, giving Raven a pat on the neck. "Not today, boy," she said, sounding apologetic. "But soon, I promise."

After returning Raven to his stall, Zoe packed up and headed for home. She knew she wouldn't see Raven again until the next day—Opening Day. Marcus had agreed to trailer the horses over to Grindlerock, so everyone could watch from the sidelines on horseback. Of course, Zoe had to go to the Race Day Banquet first in order to watch Rosie in all her glory. After all the crazy events of the week, Zoe was almost looking forward to the pomp of the Race Day festivities—the tiny morsels of food, the parade of hats, the dazzling oration by the lovely Rosie.

Soon, the race would be over. They might not have all the answers they wanted by then, but they would have the answer to the biggest question of all: Who would win the Grindlerock Classic?

10

Trouble on the Track

W hat's the deal with your oversized satchel?" Rosie said, giving Zoe's backpack the stink eye as they were heading out to the Race Day Banquet. "The rest of your ensemble is exquisite, but it demands a clutch, not a dingy duffel."

"I need this; it's my clothes for when we watch the race," Zoe reminded Rosie. "I can't wear a satin wrap dress anywhere near Raven. He would cover it with frothy drool in seconds."

"That's what you get for being a lowly commoner and watching from the sidelines," Rosie teased. "I, of course, will be in the box seats, shielded from the sun by an awning. Sipping a soda. With a prime view of the finish line."

"We can't all be the fortunate ones," Zoe responded.

"Okay," Rosie said. "As long as you stash that carryall under a table as soon as you arrive, I'll loan you one of my discreet beaded bags that you can carry around the tent. I'll get it for you, but then we have to go. The hostess cannot be tardy!"

"Today is a wonderful day for the island," Rosie said from the stage at the front of the tent. "Dare I say it's historic, as it marks the return of one of our greatest landmarks, the Grindlerock Racing Grounds. How did I not even know about this place until a few weeks ago?"

Zoe had heard Rosie rehearse the lines a thousand times, but that morning's version was clearly the best. Rosie had such a natural presence. It was as if she'd been born with a microphone in her hand! She sparkled more than the sequins on her pink spectator hat. Aster looked very pleased with her young protégé.

If the pageantry at the Race Day Banquet was any indication, Grindlerock was a raging success. The tent was full to bursting. Zoe suspected well over half the guests were from the mainland, and they no doubt felt it was worth the trip.

Colorful flags from the various participating stables hung from the tent roof. The flowers were at once quaint, like a backyard garden, and grand, like a royal wedding. "I suggested these." Zoe's mom pointed out a giant vase filled with multicolored hydrangeas to Grampa and Zoe.

Zoe had planned to approach Crispin or Mia with questions if she saw them, but neither of them showed up for the banquet. Zoe thought it was odd for Mia to miss a chance at being in the limelight. Many of the other riders were there and stood when Rosie called their names. The applause was both polite and celebratory.

But of course, the greatest sign that Grindlerock was a smashing social event was the bounty of beautiful hats. The elegant array of accessories was mind-boggling. While Zoe had admired her flapper turban in the mirror that morning, she felt she could barely tilt her head while it was on. She worried the slightest breeze would whisk it away. She swore she would take it off the second she left the buffet tent, and she did. Give her a riding helmet any day!

As soon as Rosie's duties for the day were complete, Zoe rushed over to the jockey lounge and quickly changed into her riding breeches, boots, and a crisp cotton shirt. She was anxious to meet up with Becky and Jade, but then she remembered she'd also have to confront Marcus and Raven. From what she could tell, her trainer questioned her priorities. Maybe her horse did, too.

When Zoe arrived at the trailer at the given time, everyone was there: Becky, Jade, Susie, Marcus, and the horses, including Prince!

"Good to see you, Zoe," Marcus said, without a hint of acknowledgment of their confrontation from the day before. "Raven will be glad to see you, too." Zoe gave Marcus a half smile, but as soon as she stepped into the trailer, she realized it was true. Raven whinnied. He tossed his head.

"Hey, boy," Zoe said. "Want to get out of here?" Raven pushed his muzzle against her shoulder, resting it there. "I'm happy to see you, too," she said, feeling a rush of relief.

The others had already saddled their horses but had waited for Zoe so they could walk over to the viewing area together. It was still ten or fifteen minutes to gate time, but they wanted to get a good position. Of course, most of the viewing audience would be watching from the grandstands—either the one in front of the steeplechase hurdles, or the one positioned by the homestretch, where the horses galloped for the win. They could also follow the rest of the race on monitors.

As the Bright Fields group was waiting to hear the starting gun that marked the beginning of the race, Liam approached them. Still in a grime-streaked shirt and a baseball cap, he hardly matched the rest of the crowd. Even those gathered on the greens bordering the course wore their finery. Susie was in her full show gear, with her competitive helmet and wool fitted jacket. Marcus had even shined his high boots for the event.

"Hey, Liam!" Jade said, noticing her friend emerge from the crowd. "You made it! The track looks amazing!"

But the grounds worker's smile hardly conveyed pride in a job well done. He looked tense.

"I don't know who else to talk to," he said, glancing over his shoulder as he spoke, acknowledging both Becky and Zoe, who stood close by with Bob and Raven. "I think there's something weird going on. I think someone's trying to throw the race."

"What do you mean?" Jade asked, motioning to her friends. "How?"

"I don't know exactly," he said. As soon as Zoe and Becky joined them, Liam continued. "I came to the track early, just to walk the course and make sure everything was in order, especially since it rained last night," he explained. "As I was walking past the ravine water fence, I noticed one of the contract workers there." Zoe's mind flashed to an image of the water fence in the gully.

"When I went to do the mandatory check for how much water had collected, he all out yelled at me," Liam said. "He said that I had no right to test the fence because it wasn't on my log. Then he grabbed my checklist and flipped the pages and showed me how that fence was crossed off my list. It made no sense."

Zoe glanced at Jade and Becky, trying to determine where things were headed. Waiting for Liam to continue, Zoe's heart started to pound. She looked at her watch. Seconds were ticking away. "So did you test it?" Zoe urged.

Liam shook his head. "No, he chased me away," he said. "And when I snuck back, at the end of my rounds, he was still there!"

"But why wouldn't he let you check it?" Jade asked.

"I have no idea," Liam said. "That fence has been closed off all week."

"Just a sec," Zoe said. She dug through her "carry-all," as Rosie had called it, and pulled out her mom's camera. She had brought it to take photos of everyone dressed to the nines at the banquet. She scrolled through the photos. All the while, the start of the race was being announced . . . by her sister! "Was this the guy guarding the fence?" she asked, holding the camera up for Liam.

"Yeah, that's him."

Zoe looked at Becky. "It's your bad-hair dude," Zoe said.

"I'd recognize that dye job anywhere," Becky murmured.

Zoe focused in on the photo. "What's Swamp Sand?" Zoe asked, reading the words on the bag he was holding.

"That's what he's carrying? Swamp Sand?" Liam asked.

"Yeah, is it some special soil for wet conditions?" Zoe asked.

"No, not at all," Liam said. "Swamp Sand is practically quicksand. If you used that in front of a fence, no horse could keep its footing, not at the speed they're going. The horses' hooves would just sink in, and they couldn't take off."

Zoe remembered what Jade had said about the Grand National—about how the horses ran in tight clusters, jumping the hurdles all crowded together. She pictured piles of horses in a jumble on the turf or in the pool. Jade and Becky seemed to be thinking the exact same thing, and they all exchanged looks of horror.

"You don't think he was spreading that around the water fence, do you?" Liam asked, catching on.

"Yes, Liam," Zoe said grimly. "I think that's exactly what he was doing."

Over the loudspeaker, the national anthem began to play. The start of the race was just moments away.

"So, I hate to ask, but what's the endgame?" Jade tapped her index fingers together, thinking. "If the turf in front of the fence will keep horses from clearing it, then no one finishes the race? What's the point?"

"I was trying to figure that out," Liam said. "I guess if they rigged it just right, they could make it look like most horses just couldn't make the jump. And then, maybe, there's a clear path, where the footing is good and other horses *can* clear the fence. If they did that, it'd reduce the field of competitors," Liam surmised, "by a lot."

"So only certain riders might know where the jump was safe," Zoe concluded, thinking about the gully. "Maybe farther off the rail, where it wasn't the fastest path." Only after Zoe said it did she recall her texts with Mia—how Crispin had told her not to take the turns too tight, and how Mia had laughed off his advice. Crispin *had* been trying to help Mia—not just to win but to avoid a real disaster. "Oh, no," Zoe said. "Liam, you are so right. We have to stop the race!"

Yet in that instant, the starting gun went off. A cheer rose from the stands, and a woman began to rattle off the names of horses as she commentated the race. For a moment, Zoe froze, but then she put her foot in the stirrup and pulled herself onto Raven's back. "Jade and Liam, contact the police," Zoe said. Then they were off, weaving through the crowd of people and searching for the closest entrance to the track.

Zoe scanned the scene before her. For safety reasons, the track was boarded off with a sturdy white-washed plank fence. As the lead horses began to gallop by, Zoe knew she had no time to lose. "Excuse me, excuse me!" she yelled. "Please! Out of the way!" It wasn't until she screeched that the spectators shuffled aside. She and Raven only had enough space for four strides to gain enough speed. "We can do this, boy," she encouraged. "Go!"

Raven and Zoe found their rhythm at once. Raven leaped forward, propelling himself toward the track barrier and flying over it to gasps from the crowd. They surged into the middle of a pack of horses and riders. Hooves pounding. Nostrils flaring.

Raven pulled against the bit, trying to stretch out his neck. But Zoe had never willingly let him extend to a full gallop. She always kept him in check, especially when there were fences to jump.

The other riders' elbows were in Zoe's line of vision, pumping with each swell of motion. Clumps of wet track turf whizzed by her face. Zoe leaned forward and loosened her reins, but she still held Raven back. His powerful legs thundered underneath her, and his ears were pricked forward. He pulled away from the group, and Zoe had a clear vision of the front-runners. Zoe wondered if Raven was aware of the horses in the lead, if he was straining to reach them.

As Raven approached a hedgerow, Zoe wanted to pull back, to steady his pace, but she let Raven keep his gallop. She let herself think they were just touring the track again. This time, however, they were moving at breakneck speed. Raven did not slow as he neared the fence. Instead, he gained momentum and flew over it as if the hurdle were hardly there.

As Zoe and Raven moved into the cross-country section of the course, three horses were out in front of them, all close to the inside rail. All, if Liam was correct, headed toward the sabotaged part of the water fence.

"Off the rail!" Zoe called out as they passed a bay horse. "Get off the rail! Booby-trapped fence ahead!" The horses were so close to one another that the riders' elbows nearly touched. But Zoe's warning was in vain. In the heat of competition and thundering hooves, who would listen?

As they closed in on the two lead horses, Zoe could tell by the lavender racing silks that Mia and Supersonic were in front, a couple lengths ahead of the second horse—a gray. Raven jumped the next obstacle, lengthening his stride and increasing speed all the time. "Don't jump the water fence!" Zoe yelled as they moved past the gray horse and its rider.

The course was sloping downhill. Zoe knew they were nearing the gully. Supersonic galloped ahead, fluid and elegant, gliding along the rail. How would they ever catch them in time? Zoe's legs ached, and her arms burned from holding Raven back. It was almost impossible to hold him back, so she let him go.

It was immediate. Zoe could feel Raven relax, easing into a full gallop. Raven soared. He pulled even with Supersonic in a few strides. Zoe squeezed Raven between Supersonic and the rail, nudging the other horse away.

"Mia! You can't jump the next fence! It's sabotaged! Booby-trapped!"

But Mia was laser-focused and hadn't even realized it was Zoe racing next to her.

"Stop!" Zoe yelled, seeing the water fence closing in. When Mia didn't respond, Zoe took Raven even closer, taking both Mia and Supersonic by surprise. The chestnut horse threw her head in the air with a pained whinny, her body twisting to a stop in three jagged, jolty strides.

"You can't jump this fence!" Zoe yelled at Mia between gasps. "It's rigged! Someone sabotaged it!"

"Don't be ridiculous!" Mia cried. "You're the one trying to sabotage me!" Her face was all sweat and anger.

Just then, another horse came blazing through. It was all black and had a snake insignia on its racing silks. Monty's Pet Python. The horse whizzed down the far end of the track, avoiding Mia and Zoe's confrontation on the rail. The horse went right over the water fence. The dapple gray Raven had passed came right behind. "See!" Mia said, wheeling around. "They jumped it!"

"It's safe there," Zoe tried to explain. "Not here, on the rail. It's just what Crispin said!"

"You've cost me the race!" Mia shouted, backtracking down the gully to get speed for the water hurdle.

There was no reasoning with Mia, and another horse was nearing the fence. Zoe did the only thing she could do: She dismounted. She got off Raven and stood, waving her arms, on the track. Mia followed the path Monty's Pet Python had taken and cleared the fence, but a mass of horses were approaching now.

Zoe stood her ground, stretching her arms as wide as she could. "Stand there, boy," Zoe begged. "Stand there, or all these horses are going to end up very hurt." Raven stamped his hoof with a wet thud and snorted as the other horses thundered through the gully. Raven's eyes flashed, following the parade rumbling by.

Looking down, Zoe could see Raven's hooves pressed deep into the spongy earth. She could feel it, too. Even her feet were hard to move. It might not be actual quick-sand, but it was sure close.

11

Completing the Puzzle

After Zoe, Jade, and Liam had all darted off, Becky couldn't just stand around and watch the race. "I need to do something to help!" she announced, though no one was around to hear her except Bob. "What about you, Bob?" Bob whinnied in response. Becky decided to ride back toward the trailer to find something to do. On her way, she noticed a battalion of mounted policemen who had obviously ferried over from the mainland. "Uh-oh, Bob," she said. She could only imagine that they were there on official police business. "Do you really think they'd arrest Mr. Cooke right away, before the race finishes?" Becky wondered. Bob threw his head up as if to say yes. "Well, then, we can't leave Rosie in the thick of it! Suit up, Bob, it's hero time!"

Becky figured the best way to rescue Rosie was to get as close to the box seats as possible—and she couldn't get much closer than being on the track itself.

"You can help with that," she told Bob. Plus, Becky had swung by the Bright Fields trailer to get an extra helper: Prince. The pony, who was often reluctant, seemed happy enough to trail behind Bob as they made their way through the clusters of spectators.

As they headed toward the track, Becky kept an eye out for the mounted police. She didn't see them anywhere and wondered if they were just there for crowd control. When she found an entry point to the racecourse, she steered Bob right onto the grassy track. Becky held Prince's reins, and he followed without protest. "We're going to get Rosie, and you will both be horse heroes," she promised. In the very next moment, Becky noticed a police officer on foot at the far end of the stands. He was making wild gestures at something or someone. Becky hesitantly looked over her shoulder and saw a full battalion of mounted police behind her, standing guard.

When she looked back to the other end of the stands, she noticed more mounted police. She started to wonder if they were going to arrest her for trespassing!

As far as Becky could tell, she had about thirty

seconds to get Rosie out of the stands and on Prince's back, or they would be in the middle of a dramatic arrest. "Go, Bob!" Becky yelled. Bob bounded forward, and Becky scanned the bleachers as he loped down the track, Prince at his side. "Rosie!" Becky shouted. "Rosie!"

"Oh, thank marmalade!" Becky called when she saw Rosie racing down the steps. "Quick, Zoe is having a wardrobe crisis," Becky yelled. "You have to help!"

Rosie stared at Becky in disbelief—and confusion. She looked at Prince warily. "Uh, I don't know if I can . . ."

"Hurry, Rosie!" Becky urged.

"But I'm not like Zoe!" Rosie burst out. "I can't just leap onto a horse and ride into the sunset gracefully. I don't know if I can even ride at all. I don't think I'm good at it," she finished in almost a whisper.

Becky leaned forward. "Honestly, Rosie, the police are coming and we have to skedaddle! No time for crippling self-doubt. Get on Prince now!" Becky commanded.

Rosie had never seen Becky so take-charge—and it seemed she had no choice. So she stuck one pointed, sparkly flat on the wooden fence, and threw herself onto Prince's back.

The nearby audience applauded her agility, and Prince tossed his nose in the air, certain the praise was for him.

By this time, most everyone had noticed the approaching squadron of police horses.

"Bob! Let's bolt!" Becky patted her pony's rump, and he took off. Rosie barely nudged Prince and he cantered right behind Bob as the two girls and ponies narrowly escaped the police horses closing in from both directions.

As soon as they were off the track, Rosie couldn't contain her excitement anymore. "That was actually fun!" she exclaimed. The ponies slowed to a walk, but they still gained plenty of attention from people who had seen them on the track's many monitors. Rosie sat back and enjoyed the spotlight for the second time that day. She patted Prince's neck and considered becoming more dedicated to her new favorite hobby—and her new favorite pony as well.

Corralling all the horses back into the Bright Fields trailer—Firefly included—had been a special brand of chaos, especially with the crowds of confused spectators and swarms of local police and officers who had arrived from the mainland. Jade and Liam had spent a full hour in questioning before they were allowed to leave. The investigators watched awkward footage of Zoe and Raven attempting to cordon off the inside edge of the water fence as platoons of hooves pounded past.

After the race was over, Liam walked the course with the lead detective, and they took samples of the obviously spongy soil. Neither spoke about how horrible the horses' injuries might have been if Zoe and Raven had not been able to warn the riders and steer them away from danger.

Once all horses and riders were back at Bright Fields, Mia issued Zoe a very heartfelt and public apology. "Now, if Supersonic and I hadn't managed to win, I might hold a grudge, because we really were the best team," she insisted. "Only Firefly and I would have been better."

The good news for Mia was that Firefly was perfectly healthy. Becky's suspicions had been correct: The so-called vet who had diagnosed him had not been a vet at all, but one of Mr. Cooke's hired minions. It was clear that Mr. Cooke had considered Mia and Firefly too big of a threat to his plan. Plus, Mr. Cooke had needed a new rider for Supersonic. Crispin had discovered that his father had something nefarious planned and had immediately refused to ride. "He sent me several texts of apology," Mia informed everyone. "He couldn't bring himself to show up for the race, but he didn't want any harm to come to me—or Supersonic, of course." Mia seemed to make it sound so simple, but Zoe knew that it had to be tumultuous for Crispin, finding out that his dad was planning something so horrible.

The even better news for Mia was that Zoe was feeling generous. Zoe was willing to let Mia bask in the glory of her come-from-behind win with Supersonic, even though Zoe was certain that she and Raven would have beat them by a mile. It had been very anticlimactic, chasing down the race's front-runners only to have to stop in the middle to drive all the horses away from the rigged jump. But it was worth it to keep those horses and their riders safe. And Mia's win was in title only, after all—Mr. Cooke's scheme rendered the entire race invalid, meaning no one took home the prize money after all.

Zoe could only wonder what would have happened if she and Raven had officially entered the Grindlerock Classic. It was true that Zoe had needed a break from competition, but now she hoped she had a better sense of how to do what was best for both her and Raven. Zoe couldn't hold Raven back—and she couldn't hold herself back, either.

The day after the chaos of the race, the Bright Fields

family met up in the stables office and shared the leftovers from the Race Day Banquet to celebrate Firefly and Mia's safe return—and Mr. Cooke's takedown.

"This is seriously delicious," Marcus told Rosie.

"Perhaps I'll have you plan my next birthday gathering," Mia said, flashing Rosie a smile. "And my next twelve formal dances."

"Now we're talking," Rosie said, already mentally considering various gowns for a number of occasions. "Just as long as it doesn't conflict with my riding lessons. Now that I know I can do it, I want to really commit."

"I'm glad to hear that," her mom said. "Why the sudden change of heart?"

Rosie sighed. "I was kind of worried. I mean, Zoe is super talented at riding, and, you know, Zoe and I aren't very much alike. I just thought that I might not be very good."

"Riding talent runs in the family," her mom said. "And you and Zoe are more similar than you know."

Suddenly, Jade burst in. "Look what I've got!" she announced, waving something over her head. "It's the school paper!" Jade announced. "Hot off the presses! I made the front page!"

Becky and Zoe hurried over to her side and looked

at the cover story. GRINDLEROCK: A CURSED RACING SCHEME!

"It's not at all the story that I thought I would write," Jade admitted. "I had to work all night and totally rewrite it, but I emailed the article just in time to make tomorrow's edition!"

"What was your grade?" Becky asked.

"Who cares? I made the cover with an investigative piece that includes details of Mr. Cooke's arrest on several charges," Jade exclaimed. "He won't ever be allowed to own a racehorse or work in the racing industry again." When Zoe and Becky eyed her suspiciously, Jade confessed. "Also, Mrs. Wells hinted that I'll probably get an A and loads of extra credit. I really owe you guys!"

As the three friends chatted in the corner, Zoe became uncomfortably aware that someone was watching her: her mom. She walked over to the three teenagers with her eyebrows raised. Zoe braced herself.

"So, you were just checking on Mia?" she said, repeating Zoe's claim from their earlier spying session.

"Well, it's true. We *were* worried about her," Zoe insisted, "and we were suspicious of some other things, too. But nothing made any sense at all—I mean zero sense—until today."

Zoe's mom studied her daughter's face.

"If we had figured it out any sooner, we would have told you," Zoe said, looking to her friends for support.

"You are the first adult we would have told, Mrs. Phillips," Jade declared.

"I believe you, Jade." Zoe's mom seemed to take Jade's statement as a compliment. "So, absolutely no drama, no suspicions, no spying, no bird-watching moving forward."

Becky moved to protest the last demand, but Zoe stopped her. "None of the above," Zoe promised, and she honestly hoped she could keep that promise.

"When the sheriff questioned me about Firefly, he said that the county is going to take over Grindlerock. They'll probably close the racecourse and make the mansion and grounds into a park. So don't worry, you won't have to train with me for any more local races," Mia announced. "But I read about a steeplechase in Dorset in May. That would give us tons of time to get ready. Am I right?" Mia looked around the room. "Right, Susie?"

"Right, Mia," Susie said on cue, "but you better be prepared, because Darcy and I might beat you next time."

Mia looked horrified, but Zoe was glad to see that Susie had learned how to be Mia's friend and still be true to herself.

"And you know what that means, everyone?" Becky announced happily. "The Grindlerock Curse has officially been lifted!" Jade and Zoe burst out laughing. In a way, Becky was absolutely right.

As Zoe looked around at her family and friends chattering away, she felt content—but she also felt someone was missing. She left the gathering and headed to the paddock, where Raven was snacking on some grass. She felt her pocket vibrate and pulled out her phone. As if he could read her thoughts all the way from another country—it was Pin.

Pin You still there?

Zoe Pin, I have so much to tell you.

Pin Let me guess, causing trouble again?

Zoe grinned. She couldn't wait to tell him everything! And her grin grew bigger as Raven sauntered over to her. He lifted his nose over the fence, blowing warm air into her ear. "I get it, boy," she said softly. For now, she certainly wasn't in search of any more evil plots. But she couldn't really help the fact that she and Raven were destined for adventure. It would always find them—and that was exactly how they liked it.

About the Author

Horses were all Jeanette Lane could think about while growing up in the Midwest. As soon as she started riding lessons in third grade, she found a second home at the stables—and a second family. Soon, Jeanette was spending all her spare hours at the barn with the ponies, horses, and cats—and all the amazing people who loved horses as much as she did. Now she lives in Brooklyn, New York, with her husband, two kids, and one cat. Jeanette still thinks a lot about horses, but now she more often rides the subway.

free REIN

Fight to the Finish

The adventures at Bright Field Stables continue in
Fight to the Finish! Read on for a sneak peek.

$\mathcal{E}$asy, Raven. What is it, boy?" Zoe Phillips stepped back as the big black horse she was grooming suddenly lifted his head and pawed at the floor. He was tied in his stall, so he couldn't go far. But he pricked his ears toward the door and snorted.

Zoe smiled, admiring how beautiful he was. Sometimes she still felt like pinching herself when she looked at Raven—especially when she remembered he belonged to her now. But this was a dream she never wanted to wake up from!

"Zoe!" Suddenly, Becky burst into the stall, breathless and pink-cheeked. "There you are!"

"Where else would she be, silly?" Jade stepped into view behind Becky, smiling and shaking her head. "Sorry, Raven, we didn't mean to spook you."

"He's all right." Zoe gave Raven a pat, then stepped toward her friends. Together, the three of them made up the Pony Squad. "I was about to tack him up for a ride. What's up?"

"Something utterly amazing is going to happen—right here at Bright Field Stables!" Becky exclaimed, her blond braids practically quivering with enthusiasm. "I'm serious, Zoe. This is big news! As in, big, big, big!"

"And just when things were getting back to normal around here . . ." Zoe traded a smile with Jade. The three of them had recently helped thwart a crooked race promoter who'd been up to no good.

But that wasn't the only adventure that had befallen Zoe since moving from Los Angeles to this little island off the coast of England. Her mother had grown up here, and her grandfather still lived in an old brick house just beyond the stable grounds. Ever since she had met Raven, her world had turned upside down. He'd been almost totally wild then, and she'd been the only person who was able to calm him down. That was how she'd ended up at Bright Field Stables . . . and her life had changed forever.

"Okay," she said, smiling at Becky. "What's the big news?"

"Poppy Addison!" Becky cried. "She's coming! As in, here! As in, soon! As in, O, capital M, capital Gosh!"

Before Zoe could ask who Poppy Addison was and why her arrival was so exciting, they were joined by Mia and Susie. Mia and Susie weren't Zoe's friends, exactly, but they both kept horses at Bright Fields, too. In fact, Mia had owned several horses when Zoe had first met her—including Raven. And her wealthy father, Elliott MacDonald, used to own Bright Fields.

But recently the Bright Fields stable hand, Pin Hawthorn, had discovered that he was actually a duke—and worth more money than anyone else on the island! He'd bought the stables from Mr. MacDonald and rebuilt it after a fire had destroyed much of the place. Now Pin was off traveling the world to places he never thought he'd have the money to see.

Where are you right now, Pin? Zoe wondered, her heart thumping at the thought of him. She'd felt a connection with Pin from the start, even back in his stable hand days when he'd been prickly and suspicious. In some ways, things were even more complicated now that he was a duke. They texted each other pretty often, but it was hard not having him around in person—especially since Zoe still wasn't sure exactly where they stood, relationship-wise. She couldn't wait to see him whenever he finally returned to the island for good.

In the meantime, Mia was acting a bit more humble these days—or, at least, she seemed to be trying to. Pin had bought Raven for Zoe, and Mia was back to focusing on her favorite horse, a lovely and talented gray gelding named Firefly. The two of them had been winning at shows together for years, and they had a bond almost as special as the one Zoe had with Raven.

"Did you tell Zoe about the clinic yet?" Susie asked, her blue eyes sparkling with excitement.

"I don't know why you're all so eager to tell Zoe about it." Mia wrinkled her nose as she glanced at Raven. "I mean, Raven isn't exactly a dressage horse, is he? Besides, clinics aren't meant for beginner riders."

"Huh?" Zoe looked from one girl to the next, more confused than ever. "What's a clinic? And who's this Poppy person?"

Becky's eyes widened even more. "Don't tell me you've never heard of Poppy Addison!"

Jade poked her on the shoulder. "Of course she hasn't. Zoe's still fairly new to this horse stuff, remember? Plus, she's American—Poppy probably isn't as famous over in the States."

Zoe smiled. That was pure Jade—sensible, rational, always looking for answers. She was as levelheaded and logical as Becky was happy-go-lucky and creative. And Zoe loved them both exactly the way they were.

"Well, on this island, Poppy's a total rock star," Susie declared. "Right, Mia?"

"Absolutely. That's why my father invited her to do a clinic here when he heard she and her partners had an opening in their schedule." Mia shrugged. "Naturally, he made sure I was the first rider signed up to ride."

Zoe shook her head. "Whoa, slow down, people. Still not fully up to speed on what's going on here."

"Sorry." Jade smiled. "Poppy Addison is a famous dressage rider. She grew up right here on the island—"

"With my dad," Mia broke in. "They're great friends. More like family, really—he calls her the little sister he never had."

Becky nodded. "And now she's on the national equestrian team! Like, the one going to the next Olympics! Isn't that cool?"

"Totally cool," Zoe agreed. "So is a clinic like a riding demonstration or something?"

"Almost. A clinic is more like an extended lesson," Jade explained.

"Yeah, but only if you think Oxford University is like an extended primary school!" Becky exclaimed.

"It's definitely higher riding education. Ride-u-cation? Higher-rider-cation?"

"No, Jade is exactly right." Susie jumped in. "A clinic really is like a super-intensive lesson with the best instructors around. Poppy has been traveling all over the UK with two of her fellow riders from the national dressage team. They stop at different stables, and the three of them teach a group of riders over the course of a full day at each place. It's a way for everyone to improve their skills by riding with the best, you know?"

"Oh! Cool." Zoe glanced at Raven, who was nosing at his hay net. "So can anyone sign up to ride?"

"No!" Mia said quickly. "I mean, there are a limited number of spots. So you might already be too late. Besides, it's quite expensive—much more than a regular lesson."

"Well, I've already signed up," Susie said with a happy sigh. "I can't believe the luck of Poppy coming here now of all times! Darcy and I have been focusing on our dressage ever since Junior Nationals, and Marcus says we're coming along well."

Zoe nodded. Darcy was Susie's horse, an elegant bay mare. The two of them were primarily jumpers, but Darcy was what Bright Fields's head trainer, Marcus, called an all-rounder—a horse that could do just about anything.

"Okay, all I know about dressage is that it doesn't involve jumping, which means I haven't paid that much attention to it so far," Zoe said with a laugh. "It's basically just fancy flatwork set to music, right? Like the hip-hop routine Becky and Bob did at the County Show?" Bob was the shaggy Gypsy Cob that Becky shared with her younger brother.

"There's not always music involved," Jade said. "What Becky and Bob did was called a musical freestyle."

Susie nodded. "Only a few dressage shows do that."

"Right. That's why Bob and I don't compete much," Becky added. "If there's no hip-hop involved, he tends to get bored and start inventing his own movements."

"So non-Bob dressage is fancy flatwork *without* music, then." Zoe smiled and gave Raven a rub on the neck. "Raven and I can probably handle that."

"Don't be so sure, Zoe," Mia said. "There's a lot more to dressage than just walk, trot, canter. You have to perform a test—"

"That's sort of like following a course in jumping," Susie put in helpfully. "A dressage test lays out a pattern of moves you have to ride in a certain order."

"What kinds of moves?" Zoe asked.

Mia sighed. "If you have to ask . . ."

"Bob and I can show you some moves, Zoe," Becky offered. "Dressage is sort of Bob's specialty. I'm sure Poppy will be totally impressed when she sees what he can do."

Mia snorted. "Yeah, right. I'm *so* sure that *Bob* is the one who'll catch a future Olympian's eye."

"Thanks, Becky. That would be great." Zoe traded an amused look with Jade. Bob wasn't exactly fancy—but he definitely had a lot of personality!

"By the way, you haven't even heard the best part yet," Mia added, tossing her long brown hair over one shoulder. "Poppy will be staying at my house while she's back on the island. She's even arriving a couple of days earlier than her teammates so she and my dad can catch up." She shot a smug smile around the group. "Like I said, she's practically family. It'll be such fun getting to know her better."

"Oh, lucky!" Susie cried. "Do you suppose she'll spend much time here at the yard? It would be awesome having her around for the extra couple of days!"

Becky let out a squeak. "Not just awesome— *horse-some*! I mean, a real equestrian celebrity, right here at our little stables? Wow!"